W9-BDR-521

Conn Maxwell told them: "There are incredible things still undiscovered; most of the important installations were built in duplicate as a precaution against space attack. I know where all of them are.

"But I could find nothing, not one single word, about any giant strategic planning computer called Merlin!"

Nevertheless the leading men of the planet didn't believe him. They couldn't, for the search for Merlin had become their abiding obsession. Merlin meant everything to them: power, pleasures, and profits unlimited.

Conn had known they'd never believe him, and so he had a trick or two up his space-trained sleeve that might outwit even their fabled Cosmic Computer . . . if they dared accept his challenge.

H. BEAM PIPER is rather enigmatic where his personal statistics are concerned. It may be stated that he lives in Williamsport, Pennsylvania, that he is an expert on the history and use of hand weapons, that he has been writing and selling science-fiction for many years to the leading magazines, and that he is highly rated among readers for his skill and imagination. He has had several novels published, including mysteries and juveniles.

His previous appearances in Ace Books include two novels written in collaboration with John J. McGuire: CRISIS IN 2140 (D-227) and A PLANET FOR TEXANS (D-299), and a longer entirely self-authored novel SPACE VIKING (F-225).

THE COSMIC COMPUTER

(Original Title: Junkyard Planet)

H. BEAM PIPER

ACE BOOKS, INC.
1120 Avenue of the Americas
New York, N.Y. 10036

I

THIRTY MINUTES to Litchfield.

Conn Maxwell, at the armor-glass front of the observation deck, watched the landscape rush out of the horizon and vanish beneath the ship, ten thousand feet down. He thought he knew how an hourglass must feel with the sand slowly draining out.

It had been six months to Litchfield when the *Mizar* lifted out of La Plata Spaceport and he watched Terra dwindle away. It had been two months to Litchfield when he boarded the *City of Asgard* at the port of the same name on Odin. It had been two hours to Litchfield when the *Countess Dorothy* rose from the airship dock at Storisende. He had had all that time, and now it was gone, and he was still unprepared for what he must face at home.

Thirty minutes to Litchfield.

The words echoed in his mind as though he had spoken them aloud, and then, realizing that he never addressed himself as sir, he turned. It was the first mate.

He had a clipboard in his hand, and he was wearing a Terran Federation Space Navy uniform of forty years, or about a dozen regulation-changes, ago. Once Conn had taken that sort of thing for granted. Now it was obtruding upon him everywhere.

"Thirty minutes to Litchfield, sir," the first officer repeated, and gave him the clipboard to check the luggage list. Valises, two; trunks, two; microbook case, one. The last item fanned a small flicker of anger, not at any person, not even at himself, but at the whole infernal situation. He nodded.

"That's everything. Not many passengers left aboard, are there?"

"You're the only one, first class, sir. About forty farm laborers on the lower deck." He dismissed them as mere cargo. "Litchfield's the end of the run."

"I know. I was born there."

The mate looked again at his name on the list and grinned.

"Sure; you're Rodney Maxwell's son. Your father's been giving us a lot of freight lately. I guess I don't have to tell you about Litchfield."

"Maybe you do. I've been away for six years. Tell me, are they having labor trouble now?"

"Labor trouble?" The mate was surprised. "You mean with the farm-tramps? Ten of them for every job, if you call that trouble."

"Well, I noticed you have steel gratings over the gangway heads to the lower deck, and all your crewmen are armed. Not just pistols, either."

"Oh. That's on account of pirates."

"Pirates?" Conn echoed.

"Well, I guess you'd call them that. A gang'll come aboard, dressed like farm-tramps; they'll have tommy guns and sawed-off shotguns in their bindles. When the ship's airborne and out of reach of help, they'll break out their guns and take her. Usually kill all the crew and passengers. They don't like to leave live witnesses," the mate said. "You heard about the *Harriet Barne*, didn't you?"

She was Transcontinent & Overseas, the biggest contra-gravity ship on the planet.

6

"They didn't pirate her, did they?"

The mate nodded. "Six months ago; Blackie Perales' gang. There was just a tag end of a radio call, that ended in a shot. Time the Air Patrol got to her estimated position it was too late. Nobody's ever seen ship, officers, crew or passengers since."

"Well, great Ghu; isn't the Government doing anything about it?"

"Sure. They offered a big reward for the pirates, dead or alive. And there hasn't been a single case of piracy inside the city limits of Storisende," he added solemnly.

The Calder Range had grown to a sharp blue line on the horizon ahead, and he could see the late afternoon sun on granite peaks. Below, the fields were bare and brown, and the woods were autumn-tinted. They had been green with new foliage when he had last seen them, and the wine-melon fields had been in pink blossom. Must have gotten the crop in early, on this side of the mountains. Maybe they were still harvesting, over in the Gordon Valley. Or maybe this gang below was going to the wine-pressing. Now that he thought of it, he'd seen a lot of cask staves going aboard at Storisende.

Yet there seemed to be less land under cultivation now than six years ago. He could see squares of bracken and low brush that had been melon fields recently, among the new forests that had grown up in the past forty years. The few stands of original timber towered above the second growth like hills; those trees had been there when the planet had been colonized.

That had been two hundred years ago, at the beginning of the Seventh Century, Atomic Era. The name "Poictesme" told that—Surromanticist Movement, when they were rediscovering James Branch Cabell. Old Genji Gartner, the scholarly and half-piratical space-rover whose ship had been the first to enter the Trisystem, had been devoted to the romantic writers of the Pre-Atomic Era. He had named all the planets of the Alpha System from the books of Cabell, and those of Beta from Spenser's *Faerie Queene*, and those of Gamma from Rabelais. Of course, the camp village at his first landing site on this one had been called Storisende.

Thirty years later, Genji Gartner had died there, after seeing Storisende grow to a metropolis and Poictesme become a Member Republic in the Terran Federation. The other planets were uninhabitable except in airtight dome cities, but they were rich in minerals. Companies had been formed to exploit them. No food could be produced on any of them except by carniculture and hydroponic farming, and it had been cheaper to produce it naturally on Poictesme. So Poictesme had concentrated on agriculture and had prospered. At least, for about a century.

Other colonial planets were developing their own industries; the manufactured goods the Gartner Trisystem produced could no longer find a profitable market. The mines and factories on Jurgen and Koshchei, on Britomart and Calidore, on Panurge and the moons of Pantagruel closed, and the factory workers went away. On Poictesme, the offices emptied, the farms contracted, forests reclaimed fields, and the wild game came back.

Coming toward the ship out of the east, now, was a vast desert of crumbling concrete—landing fields and parade grounds, empty barracks and toppling sheds, airship docks, stripped gun emplacements and missile-launching sites. These were more recent, and dated from Poictesme's second hectic prosperity, when the Gartner Trisystem had been the advance base for the Third Fleet-Army Force, during the System States War.

It had lasted twelve years. Millions of troops were stationed on or routed through Poictesme. The mines and factories reopened for war production. The Federation spent trillions on trillions of sols, piled up mountains of supplies and equipment, left the face of the world cluttered with installations. Then, without warning, the System States Alliance collapsed, the rebellion ended, and the scourge of peace fell on Poictesme.

The Federation armies departed. They took the clothes they stood in, their personal weapons, and a few souvenirs. Everything else was abandoned. Even the most expensive equipment had been worth less than the cost of removal.

The people who had grown richest out of the War had

followed, taking their riches with them. For the next forty years, those who remained had been living on leavings. On Terra, Conn had told his friends that his father was a prospector, leaving them to interpret that as one who searched, say, for uranium. Rodney Maxwell found quite a bit of uranium, but he got it by taking apart the warheads of missiles.

Now he was looking down on the granite spines of the Calder Range; ahead the misty Gordon Valley sloped and widened to the north. Twenty minutes to Litchfield, now. He still didn't know what he was going to tell the people who would be waiting for him. No; he knew that; he just didn't know how. The ship swept on, ten miles a minute, tearing through thin puffs of cloud. Ten minutes. The Big Bend was glistening redly in the sunlit haze, but Litchfield was still hidden inside its curve. Six. Four. The *Countess Dorothy* was losing speed and altitude. Now he could see it, first a blur and then distinctly. The Airlines Building, so thick as to look squat for all its height. The yellow block of the distilleries under their plume of steam. High Garden Terrace; the Mall.

Moment by moment, the stigmata of decay became more evident. Terraces empty or littered with rubbish; gardens untended and choked with wild growth; blank-staring windows, walls splotched with lichens. At first, he was horrified at what had happened to Litchfield in six years. Then he realized that the change had been in himself. He was seeing it with new eyes, as it really was.

The ship came in five hundred feet above the Mall, and he could see cracked pavements sprouting grass, statues askew on their pedestals, waterless fountains. At first he thought one of them was playing, but what he had taken for spray was dust blowing from the empty basin. There was a thing about dusty fountains, some poem he'd read at the University.

The fountains are dusty in the Graveyard of Dreams;
The hinges are rusty, they swing with tiny screams.

Was Poictesme a Graveyard of Dreams? No; Junkyard of

Empire. The Terran Federation had impoverished a hundred planets, devastated a score, actually depopulated at least three, to keep the System States Alliance from seceding. It hadn't been a victory. It had only been a lesser defeat.

There was a crowd, almost a mob, on the dock; nearly everybody in topside Litchfield. He spotted old Colonel Zareff, with his white hair and plum-brown skin, and Tom Brangwyn, the town marshal, red-faced and bulking above everybody else. Kurt Fawzi, the mayor, well to the front. Then he saw his father and mother, and his sister Flora, and waved to them. They waved back, and then everybody was waving. The gangway-port opened, and the Academy band struck up, enthusiastically if inexpertly, as he descended to the dock.

His father was wearing a black suit with a long coat, cut to the same pattern as the one he had worn six years ago. Blackout curtain cloth. It was fairly new, but the coat had begun to acquire a permanent wrinkle across the right hip, over the pistol butt. His mother's dress was new, and so was Flora's, made for the occasion. He couldn't be sure just which of the Federation Armed Forces had provided the material, but his father's shirt was Med Service sterilon.

Ashamed to be noticing things like that, he clasped his father's hand, kissed his mother, embraced his sister. There were a few, but very few, gray threads in his father's mustache; a few more squint-wrinkles around the eyes. His mother's hair was all gray, now, and she was heavier. She seemed shorter, but that would be because he'd grown a few inches in the last six years. For a moment, he was surprised that Flora actually looked younger. Then he realized that to seventeen, twenty-three is practically middle age, but to twenty-three, twenty-nine is almost contemporary. He noticed the glint on her left hand and caught it to look at the ring.

"Hey! Zarathustra sunstone! Nice," he said. "Where is he, Sis?"

He'd never met her fiancé; Wade Lucas hadn't come to Litchfield to practice medicine until the year after he'd gone to Terra.

10

"Oh, emergency," Flora said. "Obstetrical case; that won't wait on anything. In Tramptown, of course. But he'll be at the party . . . Oops, I shouldn't have said that; that's supposed to be a surprise."

"Don't worry; I'll be surprised," he promised.

Then Kurt Fawzi was pushing forward, holding out his hand. Thinner, and grayer, but just as effusive as ever.

"Welcome home, Conn. Judge, shake hands with him and tell him how glad we all are to see him back. . . . Now, Franz, put away the recorder; save the interview for the *Chronicle* till later. Ah, Professor Kellton; one pupil Litchfield Academy can be proud of!"

He shook hands with them: Judge Ledue, Franz Veltrin, old Professor Dolf Kellton. They were all happy; how much, he wondered, because he was Conn Maxwell, Rodney Maxwell's son, home from Terra, and how much because of what they hoped he'd tell them. Kurt Fawzi, edging him aside, was the first to speak of it.

"Conn, what did you find out?" he whispered. "Do you know where it is?"

He stammered, then saw Tom Brangwyn and Colonel Klem Zareff approaching, the older man tottering on a silver-headed cane and the younger keeping pace with him. Neither of them had been born on Poictesme. Tom Brangwyn had always been reticent about where he came from, but Hathor was a good guess. There had been political trouble on Hathor twenty years ago; the losers had had to get off-planet in a hurry to dodge firing squads. Klem Zareff never was reticent about his past. He came from Ashmodai, one of the System States planets, and he had commanded a regiment, and finally a division that had been blasted down to less than regimental strength, in the Alliance Army. He always wore a little rosette of System States black and green on his coat.

"Hello, boy," he croaked, extending a hand. "Good to see you again."

"It sure is, Conn," the town marshal agreed, then lowered his voice. "Find out anything definite?"

"We didn't have much time, Conn," Kurt Fawzi said, "but

11

we've arranged a little celebration for you. We'll start it with a dinner at Senta's."

"You couldn't have done anything I'd have liked better, Mr. Fawzi. I'd have to have a meal at Senta's before I'd really feel at home."

"Well, it'll be a couple of hours. Suppose we all go up to my office, in the meantime. Give the ladies a chance to fix up for the party, and have a little drink and a talk together."

"You want to do that, Conn?" his father asked. There was an odd undernote of anxiety, or reluctance, in his voice.

"Yes, of course. I'd like that."

His father turned to speak to his mother and Flora. Kurt Fawzi was speaking to his wife, interrupting himself to shout instructions to some laborers who were bringing up a contragravity skid. Conn turned to Colonel Zareff.

"Good melon crop this year?" he asked.

The old Rebel cursed. "Gehenna of a big crop; we're up to our necks in melons. This time next year we'll be washing our feet in brandy."

"Hold onto it and age it; you ought to see what they charge for a drink of Poictesme brandy on Terra."

"This isn't Terra, and we aren't selling it by the drink," Colonel Zareff said. "We're selling it at Storisende Spaceport, for what the freighter captains pay us. You've been away too long, Conn. You've forgotten what it's like to live in a poor-house."

The cargo was coming off, now. Cask staves, and more cask staves. Zareff swore bitterly at the sight, and then they started toward the wide doors of the shipping floor, inside the Airlines Building. Outgoing cargo was beginning to come out; casks of brandy, of course, and a lot of boxes and crates, painted light blue and bearing the yellow trefoil of the Third Fleet-Army Force and the eight-pointed red star of Ordnance. Cases of rifles; square boxes of ammunition; crated auto-cannon. Conn turned to his father.

"This our stuff?" he asked. "Where did you dig it?"

Rodney Maxwell laughed. "You know the old Tenth Army Headquarters, over back of Snagtooth, in the Calders? Everybody knows that was cleaned out years ago. Well, always take a second look at these things everybody knows. Ten to one they're not so. It always bothered me that nobody found any underground attack-shelters. I took a second look, and sure enough, I found them, right underneath, mined out of the solid rock. Conn, you'd be surprised at what I found there."

"Where are you going to sell that stuff?" he asked, pointing at a passing skid. "There's enough combat equipment around now to outfit a private army for every man, woman and child in Poictesme."

"Storisende Spaceport. The freighter captains buy it, and sell it on some of the planets that were colonized right before the War and haven't gotten industrialized yet. I'm clearing about two hundred sols a ton on it."

The skid at which he had pointed was loaded with cases of M504 submachine guns. Even used, one was worth fifty sols. Allowing for packing weight, his father was selling those tommy guns for less than a good café on Terra got for one drink of Poictesme brandy.

II

HE HAD BEEN in Kurt Fawzi's office before, once or twice, with his father; he remembered it as a dim, quiet place of genteel conviviality and rambling conversation. None of the lights were bright, and the walls were almost invisible in the shadows. As they entered, Tom Brangwyn went to the long table and took off his belt and holster, laying it down. One by one, the others unbuckled their weapons and added them to the pile. Klem Zareff's cane went on the table with his pistol; there was a sword inside it.

That was something else he was seeing with new eyes. He hadn't started carrying a gun when he had left for Terra, and he was wondering, now, why any of them bothered to. Why, there wouldn't be a shooting a year in Litchfield, if you didn't count the Tramptowners, and they stayed south of the docks and off the top level.

Or perhaps that was just it. Litchfield was peaceful because everybody was prepared to keep it that way. It certainly wasn't because of anything the Planetary Government did to maintain order.

Now Brangwyn was setting out glasses, filling a pitcher from a keg in the corner of the room. The last time Conn had been here, they'd given him a glass of wine, and he'd felt very grown-up because they didn't water it for him.

"Well, gentlemen," Kurt Fawzi was saying, "let's have a toast to our returned friend and new associate. Conn, we're all anxious to hear what you've found out, but even if you didn't learn anything, we're still happy to have you back with us. Gentlemen; to our friend and neighbor. Welcome home, Conn!"

"Well, it's wonderful to be back, Mr. Fawzi," he began.

"Here, none of this mister foolishness; you're one of us, now, Conn. And drink up, everybody. We have plenty of brandy, if we don't have anything else."

"You can say that again, Kurt." That was one of the distillery people; he'd remember the name in a moment. "When this new crop gets pressed and fermented . . ."

"I don't know where in Gehenna I'm going to vat mine till it ferments," Klem Zareff said.

"Or why," another planter added. "Lorenzo, what are you going to be paying for wine?"

Lorenzo Menardes; that was the name. The distiller said he was worrying about what he'd be able to get for brandy.

"Oh, please," Fawzi interrupted. "Not today; not when our boy's home and is going to tell us how we can solve all our problems."

"Yes, Conn." That was Morgan Gatworth, the lawyer. "You did find out where Merlin is, didn't you?"

That set them all off. He was still holding his drink; he downed it in one gulp, barely tasting it, and handed the glass to Tom Brangwyn for a refill, and caught a frown on his father's face. One did not gulp drinks in Kurt Fawzi's office.

Well, neither did one blast everybody's hopes with half a dozen words, and that was what he was trying to force himself to do. He wanted to blurt out the one quick sentence

14

and get it over with, but the words wouldn't come out of his throat. He lowered the second drink by half; the brandy was beginning to warm him and dissolve the cold lump in his stomach. Have to go easy, though. He wasn't used to this kind of drinking, and he wanted to stay sober enough to talk sense until he'd told them what he had to.

"I hope," he said, "that you don't expect me to show you the cross on the map, where the computer is buried."

All the eyes around him began to look troubled. Most of them had been expecting precisely that. His father was watching him anxiously.

"But it's still here on Poictesme, isn't it?" one of the melon planters asked. "They didn't take it away with them?"

"Most of you gentlemen," he said, "contributed to sending me to school on Terra, to study cybernetics and computer theory. It wouldn't do us any good to find Merlin if none of us could operate it. Well, I've done that. I can use any known type of computer, and train assistants. After I graduated, I was offered a junior instructorship in computer physics at the University."

"You didn't mention that, son," his father said.

"The letter would have come on the same ship I did. Besides, I didn't think it was very important."

"I think it is." There was a catch in old Dolf Kellton's voice. "One of my boys from the Academy offered a place on the faculty of the University of Montevideo, on Terra!" He finished his drink and held out his glass for more, something he almost never did.

"Conn means," Kurt Fawzi explained, "that it had nothing to do with Merlin."

All right; now tell them the truth.

"I was also to find out anything I could about a secret giant computer used during the War by the Third Fleet-Army Force, code-named Merlin. I went over all the records available to the public; I used your letter, Professor, and the head of our Modern History department secured me access to non-public material, some of it still classified. For one thing, I have locations and maps and plans of every Federation installation built here between 842 and 854, the whole period of the War." He turned to his father. "There are incredible things still undiscovered; most of the important installations were built in duplicate, sometimes triplicate, as a precaution against space attack. I know where all of them are."

"Space attack!" Klem Zareff was indignant. "There never was a time we could have attacked Poictesme. Even if we'd had the ships, we were fighting a purely defensive war. Aggression was no part of our policy—"

He interrupted: "Excuse me, Colonel. The point I was trying to make is that, with all I was able to learn, I could find nothing, not one single word, about any giant strategic planning computer called Merlin, or any Merlin Project."

There! He'd gotten that out. Now go on and tell them about the old man in the dome-house on Luna. The room was silent, except for the small insectile hum of the electric clock. Then somebody set a glass on the table, and it sounded like a hammer blow.

"Nothing, Conn?"

Kurt Fawzi was incredulous. Judge Ledue's hand shook as though palsied as he tried to relight his cigar. Dolf Kellton was looking at the drink in his hand as though he had no idea what it was. The others found their voices, one by one.

"Of course, it was the most closely guarded secret . . ."

"But after forty years . . ."

"Hah, don't tell me about security!" Colonel Zareff barked. "You should have seen the lengths our staff went to. I remember, once, on Mephistopheles . . ."

"But there *was* a computer code-named Merlin," Judge Ledue was insisting, to convince himself more than anybody else. "Its memory-bank contained all human knowledge. It was capable of scanning all its data instantaneously, and combining, and forming associations, and reasoning with absolute accuracy, and extrapolating to produce new facts, and predicting future events, and . . ."

And if you'd asked such a computer, "Is there a God?" it would have simply answered, "Present."

"We'd have won the War, except for Merlin," Zareff was declaring.

"Conn, from what you've learned of computers generally,

how big would Merlin have to be?" old Professor Kellton asked.

"Well, the astrophysics computer at the University occupied a volume of a hundred thousand cubic feet. For all Merlin was supposed to do, I'd say something of the order of three million to five million."

"Well, it's a cinch they didn't haul that away with them," Lester Dawes, the banker, said.

"Oh, lots of places on Poictesme where they could have hid a thing like that," Tom Brangwyn said. "You know, a planet's a mighty big place."

"It doesn't have to be on Poictesme, even," Morgan Gatworth pointed out. "It could be anywhere in the Trisystem."

"You know where I'd have put it?" Lorenzo Menardes asked. "On one of the moons of Pantagruel."

"But that's in the Gamma System, three light years away," Kurt Fawzi objected. "There isn't a hypership on this planet, and it would take half a lifetime to get there on normal-space drive."

Conn was lifting his glass to his lips. He set it down again and rose to his feet.

"Then," he said, "we will build a hypership. On Koshchei there are shipyards and hyperdrive engines and everything we will need. We only need one normal-space interplanetary ship to get out there, and we're in business."

"Well, I don't know we need one," Judge Ledue said. "That was only an idea of Lorenzo's. I think Merlin's right here on Poictesme."

"We don't know it is," Conn replied. "And we don't know we won't need a ship. Merlin may be on Koshchei; that's where the components would be fabricated, and the Armed Forces weren't hauling anything any farther than they had to. Koshchei's only two and a half minutes away by radio; that's practically in the next room. Look; here's how they could have done it."

He went on talking, about remote controls and radio transmission and positronic brains and neutrino-circuits. They believed it all, even the little they understood. They would

17

believe anything he told them about Merlin—except the truth.

"But this will take money," Lester Dawes said. "And after that infernal deluge of unsecured paper currency thirty years ago . . ."

"I have no doubt," Judge Ledue began, "that the Planetary Government at Storisende would give assistance. I have some slight influence with President Vyckhoven . . ."

"Huh-*uh!*" That was one of Klem Zareff's fellow planters. "We don't want Jake Vyckhoven or any of this First-Families-of-Storisende oligarchy in this at all. That's the gang that bankrupted the Government with doles and work relief, and everybody else with worthless printing-press money after the War, and they've been squatting in a circle deploring things ever since. Some of these days Blackie Perales and his pirates'll sack Storisende, for all they'd be able to do to stop him."

"We get a ship out to Koshchei, and the next thing you know we'll be the Planetary Government," Tom Brangwyn said.

Rodney Maxwell finished the brandy in his glass and set it on the table, then went to the pile of belts and holsters and began rummaging for his own. Kurt Fawzi looked up in surprise.

"Rod, you're not leaving are you?" he asked.

"Yes. It's only half an hour till time for dinner, and I think Conn and I ought to have a little fresh air. Besides, you know, we haven't seen each other for six years." He buckled on the heavy automatic and settled the belt over his hips. "You didn't have a gun, did you, Conn?" he asked. "Well, let's go."

III

IT WASN'T until they were down to the main level and outside in the little plaza to the east of the Airlines Building that his father broke the silence.

"That was quite a talk you gave them, Conn. They believed every word of it. I even caught myself starting to believe it once or twice."

Conn stopped short; his father halted beside him. "Why didn't you tell them the truth, son?" Rodney Maxwell asked.

The question, which he had been throwing at himself, angered him. "Why didn't I just grab a couple of pistols and shoot the lot of them?" he retorted. "It wouldn't have killed them any deader, and it wouldn't have hurt as much."

"There is no Merlin. Is that it?"

He realized, suddenly, that his father had known, or suspected that all along. He started to say something, then checked himself and began again:

"There never was one. I was going to tell them, but you saw them. I couldn't."

"You're sure of it?"

"The whole thing's a myth. I'm quoting the one man in the Galaxy who ought to know. The man who commanded the Third Force here during the War."

"Foxx Travis!" His father's voice was soft with wonder. "I saw him once, when I was eight years old. I thought he'd died long ago. Why, he must be over a hundred."

"A hundred and twelve. He's living on Luna; low gravity's all that keeps him alive."

"And you talked to him?"

"Yes."

There'd been a girl in his third-year biophysics class; he'd found out that she was a great-granddaughter of Force General Travis. It had taken him until his senior midterm vacation to wangle an invitation to the dome-house on Luna. After that, it had been easy. As soon as Foxx Travis had learned that one of his great-granddaughter's guests was from Poictesme, he had insisted on talking to him.

"What did he tell you?"

The old man had been incredibly thin and frail. Under normal gravitation, his life would have gone out like a blown match. Even at one-sixth G, it had cost him effort to rise and greet the guest. There had been a younger man, a mere stripling of seventy-odd; he had been worried, and excused himself at once. Travis had laughed after he had gone out.

19

"Mike Shanlee; my aide-de-camp on Poictesme. Now he thinks he's my keeper. He'll have a squad of doctors and a platoon of nurses in here as soon as you're gone, so take your time. Now, tell me how things are on Poictesme. . . ."

"Just about that," he told his father. "I finally mentioned Merlin, as an old legend people still talked about. I was ashamed to admit anybody really believed in it. He laughed, and said, 'Great Ghu, is that thing still around? Well, I suppose so; it was all through the Third Force during the War. Lord only knows how these rumors start among troops. We never contradicted it; it was good for morale.'"

They had started walking again, and were out on the Mall; the sky was flaming red and orange from high cirrus clouds in the sunset light. They stopped by a dry fountain, perhaps the one from which he had seen the dust blowing. Rodney Maxwell sat down on the edge of the basin and got out two cigars, handing one to Conn, who produced his lighter.

"Conn, they wouldn't have believed you *and* Foxx Travis," he said. "Merlin's a religion with those people. Merlin's a robot god, something they can shove all their problems onto. As soon as they find Merlin, everybody will be rich and happy, the Government bonds will be redeemed at face value plus interest, the paper money'll be worth a hundred Federation centisols to the sol, and the leaves and wastepaper will be raked off the Mall, all by magic." He muttered an unprintability and laughed bitterly.

"I didn't know you were the village atheist, Father."

"In a religious community, the village atheist keeps his doubts to himself. I have to do business with these Merlinolators. It's all I can do to keep Flora from antagonizing them at school."

Flora was a teacher; now she was assistant principal of the grade schools. Professor Kellton was also school superintendent. He could see how that would be.

"Flora's not a True Believer, then?"

Rodney Maxwell shook his head. "That's largely Wade Lucas's influence, I'd say. You know about him."

Just from letters. Wade Lucas was from Baldur; he'd

gone off-planet as soon as he'd gotten his M.D. Evidently the professional situation there was the same as on Terra; plenty of opportunities, and fifty competitors for each one. On Poictesme, there were few opportunities, but nobody competed for anything, not even to find Merlin.

"He'd never heard of Merlin till he came here, and when he did, he just couldn't believe in it. I don't blame him. I've heard about it all my life, and I can't."

"Why not?"

"To begin with, I suppose, because it's just another of these things everybody believes. Then, I've had to do some studying on the Third Force occupation of Poictesme to know where to go and dig, and I never found any official, or even reliably unofficial, mention of anything of the sort. Forty years is a long time to keep a secret, you know. And I can't see why they didn't come back for it after the pressure to get the troops home was off, or why they didn't build a dozen Merlins. This isn't the only planet that has problems they can't solve for themselves."

"What's Mother's attitude on Merlin?"

"She's against it. She thinks it isn't right to make machines that are smarter than people."

"I'll agree. It's scientifically impossible."

"That's what I've been trying to tell her. Conn, I noticed that after Kurt Fawzi started talking about how long it would take to get to the Gamma System, you jumped right into it and began talking up a ship. Did you think that if you got them started on that it would take their minds off Merlin?"

"That gang up in Fawzi's office? Nifflheim, no! They'll go on hunting Merlin till they die. But I was serious about the ship. An idea hit me. You gave it to me; you and Klem Zareff."

"Why, I didn't say a word . . ."

"Down on the shipping floor, before we went up. You were talking about selling arms and ammunition at a profit of two hundred sols a ton, and Klem was talking as though a bumper crop was worse than a Green Death epidemic. If we had a hypership, look what we could do. How much do you think a settler on Hoth or Malebolge or Irminsul would pay for a good rifle and a thousand rounds? How much would he pay for his life?—that's what it would come to. And do you know what a fifteen-cc liqueur glass of Poictesme brandy sells for on Terra? One sol; Federation money. I'll admit it costs like Nifflheim to run a hypership, but look at the difference between what these tramp freighter captains pay at Storisende and what they get."

"I've been looking at it for a long time. Maybe if we had a few ships of our own, these planters would be breaking new ground instead of cutting their plantings, and maybe we'd get some money on this planet that was worth something. You have a good idea there, son. But maybe there's an angle to it you haven't thought of."

Conn puffed slowly at the cigar. Why couldn't they grow tobacco like this on Terra? Soil chemicals, he supposed; that wasn't his subject.

"You can't put this scheme over on its own merits. This gang wouldn't lift a finger to build a hypership. They've completely lost hope in everything but Merlin."

"Well, can do. I'll even convince them that Merlin's a space-station, in orbit off Koshchei. I think I could do that."

"You know what it'll cost? If you go ahead with it, I'm in it with you, make no mistake about that. But you and I will be the only two people on Poictesme who can be trusted with the truth. We'll have to lie to everybody else, with every word we speak. We'll have to lie to Flora, and we'll have to lie to your mother. Your mother most of all. She believes in absolutes. Lying is absolutely wrong, no matter whom it helps; telling the truth is absolutely right, no matter how much damage it does or how many hearts it breaks. You think this is going to be worth a price like that?"

"Don't you?" he demanded, and then pointed along the crumbling and littered Mall. "Look at that. Pretend you never saw it before and are looking at it for the first time. And then tell me whether it'll be worth it or not."

His father took a cigar from his mouth. For a moment, he sat staring silently.

"Great Ghu!" Rodney Maxwell turned. "I wonder how

that sneaked up on me; I honestly never realized . . . Yes, Conn. This is a cause worth lying for." He looked at his watch. "We ought to be starting for Senta's, but let's take a few minutes and talk this over. How are you going to get it started?"

"Well, convince them that I can find Merlin and that they can't find it without me. I think I've done that already. Then convince them that we'll have to have a ship to get to Koshchei, and—"

"Won't do. That'll take money, and money's something none of this gang has."

"You heard me talk about the stuff I found out on Terra? Father, you have no idea what all there is. You remember the old Force Command Headquarters, the one the Planetary Government took over? I know where there's a duplicate of that, completely underground. It has everything the other one had, and a lot more, because it'll be cram-full of supplies to be used in case of a general blitz that would knock out everything on the planet. And a chain of hospitals. And a spaceport, over on Barathrum, that was built inside the crater of an extinct volcano. There won't be any hyperships there of course, but there'll be equipment and material. We might be able to build a ship there. And supply depots, all over the planet; none of them has ever been opened since the War. Don't worry about financing; we have that."

His father, he could see, appreciated what he had brought home from Terra. He was nodding, with quick head jerks, at each item.

"That'll do it, all right. Now, listen; what we want to do is get a company organized, a regular limited-liability company, with a charter. We'll contribute the information you brought back from Terra, and we'll get the rest of this gang to put all the money we can twist out of them into it, so we'll be sure they won't say, 'Aw, Nifflheim with it!' and walk out on us as soon as the going gets a little tough." Rodney Maxwell got to his feet, hitching his gun-belt. "I'll pass the word to Kurt to get a meeting set up for tomorrow afternoon."

"What'll we call this company? Merlin Rediscovery, Ltd?"

"No! We keep Merlin out of it. As far as the public is supposed to know, this is just a war-material prospecting company. I'll impress on them that Merlin is to be kept a secret. That way, we'll have to engage in regular prospecting and salvage work as a front. I'll see to it that the front is also the main objective." He nodded down the Mall, toward the sunset, which was blazing even higher and redder. "Well, let's go. You don't want to be late for your own welcome-home party."

They walked slowly, still talking, until they came to the end of the Mall. The escalators to the level below weren't working. Now that he thought of it, they hadn't been when he had gone away, six years ago, but he could remember riding up and down on them as a small child. For a moment they stood in the sunset light, looking down on the lower terrace as they finished their cigars.

Senta's was mostly outdoors, the tables under the open sky. The people gathered below were looking at the sunset, too; Litchfielders loved to watch sunsets, maybe because a sunset was one of the few things economic conditions couldn't affect. There was Kurt Fawzi, the center of a group to whom he was declaiming earnestly; there was his mother, and Flora, and Flora's fiancé, who was the uncomfortable lone man in an excited feminine flock. And there was Senta herself, short and dumpy, in one of her preposterous red and purple dresses, bubbling happily one moment and screaming invective at some laggard waiter the next.

They threw away their cigars and started down the long, motionless escalator. Conn Maxwell, Hero of the Hour, marching to Destiny. He seemed to hear trumpets sounding before him.

And an occasional muted Bronx cheer.

IV

THE ALARM chimed softly beside his bed; he reached out and silenced it, and lay looking at the early sunlight in the windows, and found that he was wishing himself back in his dorm room at the University. No, back in this room, ten years ago, before any of this had started. For a while, he imagined himself thirteen years old and knowing everything he knew now, and he began mapping a campaign to establish himself as Litchfield's Juvenile Delinquent Number One, to the end that Kurt Fawzi and Dolf Kellton and the rest of them would never dream of sending him to school on Terra to find out where Merlin was.

But he couldn't even go back to yesterday afternoon in Kurt Fawzi's office and tell them the truth. All he could do was go ahead. It had seemed so easy, when he and his father had been talking on the Mall; just get a ship built, and get out to Koshchei, and open some of the shipyards and engine works there, and build a hypership. Sure; easy—once he got started.

He climbed out of bed, knuckled the sleep-sand out of his eyes, threw his robe around him, and started across the room to the bath cubicle.

They had decided to have breakfast together his first morning home. The party had broken up late, and then there had been the excitement of opening the presents he had brought back from Terra. Nobody had had a chance to talk about Merlin, or about what he was going to do, now that he was home. That, and his career of mendacity, would start at breakfast. He wanted to let his father get to the table first, to run interference for him; he took his time with his toilet and dressed carefully and slowly. Finally, he zipped up the short waist-length jacket and went out.

His father and mother and Flora were at the table, and the serving-robot was floating around a few inches off the floor, steam trailing from its coffee urn and its tray lid up to offer food. He greeted everybody and sat down at his place, and the robot came around to him. His mother had selected all the things he'd been most fond of six years ago: shovel-snout bacon, hotcakes, starberry jam, things he hadn't tasted since he had gone away. He filled his plate and poured a cup of coffee.

"You don't want to bother coming out to the dig with me this morning, do you?" his father was saying. "I'll be back here for lunch, and we'll go to the meeting in the afternoon."

"Meeting?" Flora asked. "What meeting?"

"Oh, we didn't have time to tell you," Rodney Maxwell said. "You know, Conn brought back a lot of information on locations of supply depots and things like that. An amazing list of things that haven't been discovered yet. It's going to be too much for us to handle alone; we're organizing a company to do it. We'll need a lot of labor, for one thing; jobs for some of these Tramptowners."

"That's going to be something awfully big," his mother said dubiously. "You never did anything like that before."

"I never had the kind of a partner I have now. It's Maxwell & Son, from now on."

"Who's going to be in this company?" Flora wanted to know.

"Oh, everybody around town; Kurt and the Judge and Klem, and Lester Dawes. All that crowd."

"The Fawzis' Office Gang," Flora said disparagingly. "I suppose they'll want Conn to take them right to where Merlin is, the first thing."

"Well, not the first thing," Conn said. "Merlin was one thing I couldn't find out anything about on Terra."

"I'll bet you couldn't!"

"The people at Armed Forces Records would let me look at everything else, and make microcopies and all, but not one word about computers. Forty years, and they still have the security lid welded shut on that."

Flora looked at him in shocked surprise. "You don't mean to tell me you believe in that thing?"

"Sure. How do you think they fought a war around a perimeter of close to a thousand light-years? They couldn't do all that out of their heads. They'd have to have computers, and the one they'd use to correlate everything and work out grand-strategy plans would have to be a dilly. Why, I'd give anything just to look at the operating panels for that thing."

"But that's just a silly story; there never was anything like Merlin. No wonder you couldn't find out about it. You were looking for something that doesn't exist, just like all these old cranks that sit around drinking brandy and mooning about what Merlin's going to do for them, and never doing anything for themselves."

"Oh, they're going to do something, now, Flora," his father told her. "When we get this company organized—"

"You'll dig up a lot of stuff you won't be able to sell, like that stuff you've been bringing in from Tenth Army, and then you'll go looping off chasing Merlin, like the rest of them. Well, maybe that'll be a little better than just sitting in Kurt Fawzi's office talking about it, but not much."

It kept on like that. Conn and his father tried several times to change the subject; each time Flora ignored the effort and returned to her diatribe. Finally, she put her plate and cup on the robot's tray and got to her feet.

"I have to go," she said. "Maybe I can do something to keep some of these children from growing up to be Merlin-worshipers like their parents."

She flung out of the room angrily. Mrs. Maxwell looked after her in distress.

"And I thought it was going to be so nice, having breakfast together again," she lamented.

Somehow the breakfast wasn't quite as good as he'd thought it was at first. He wondered how many more breakfasts like that he was going to have to sit through. He and his father finished quickly and got up, while his mother started the robot to clearing the table.

"Conn," she said, after his father had gone out, "you shouldn't have gotten Flora started like that."

"I didn't get Flora started; she's equipped with a self-starter. If she doesn't believe in Merlin, that's her business. A lot of these people do, and I'm going to help them hunt for it. That's why they all chipped in to send me to school on Terra; remember?"

"Yes, I know." Her voice was heavy with distress. "Conn, do you really believe there is a . . . that thing?" she asked.

"Why, of course." He was mildly surprised at how sincerely and straightforwardly he said it. "I don't know where it is, but it's somewhere on Poictesme, or in the Alpha System."

"Well, do you think it would be a good thing to find it?"

That surprised him. Everybody knew it would be, and his mother didn't share his father's attitude about things everybody knew. She hadn't **any** business questioning a fundamental postulate like that.

"It frightens me," she continued. "I don't even like to think about it. A soulless intelligence; it seems evil to me."

"Well, of course it's soulless. It's a machine, isn't it? An aircar's soulless, but you're not afraid to ride in one."

"But this is different. A machine that can think. Conn, people weren't meant to make machines like that, wiser than they are."

"Now wait a minute, Mother. You're talking to a computerman now." Professional authority was something his mother oughtn't to question. "A computer like Merlin isn't intelligent, or wise, or anything of the sort. It doesn't think; the people who make computers and use them do the thinking. A computer's a tool, like a screwdriver; it has to have a man to use it."

"Well, but . . ."

"And please, don't talk about what people are *meant* to do. People aren't *meant* to do things; they *mean* to do things, and nine times out of ten, they end by doing them. It may take a hundred thousand years from a Stone Age savage in a cave to the captain of a hyperspace ship, but sooner or later they get there."

His mother was silent. The soulless machine that had been clearing the table floated out of the room, the dishwasher in its rectangular belly gurgling. Maybe what he had told her was logical, but women aren't impressed by logic. She knew better—for the good old feminine reason, *Because*.

"Wade Lucas wanted me to drop in on him for a checkup," he mentioned. "That's rubbish; I had one for my landing pratique on the ship. He just wants to size up his future brother-in-law."

"Well, you ought to go see him."

"How did Flora come to meet him, anyhow?"

"Well, you know, he came from Baldur. He was in Storisende, looking for an opening to start a practice, and he heard about some medical equipment your father had found somewhere and came out to see if he could buy it. Your father and Judge Ledue and Mr. Fawzi talked him into opening his office here. Then he and Flora got acquainted . . ." She asked, anxiously: "What did you think of him, Conn?"

"Seems like a regular guy. I think I'll like him." A husband like Wade Lucas might be a good thing for Flora. "I'll drop in on him, sometime this morning."

His mother went toward the rear of the house—more soulless machines, like the housecleaning-robot, and the laundry-robot, to look after. He went into his father's office and found the cigar humidor, just where it had been when he'd stolen cigars out of it six years ago and thought his father never suspected what he was doing.

Now, why didn't they export this tobacco? It was better than anything they grew on Terra; well, at least it was different, just as Poictesme brandy was different from Terran bourbon or Baldur honey-rum. That was the sort of thing that could be sold in interstellar trade anytime and anywhere; the luxury goods that were unique. Staple foodstuffs, utility textiles, metal products, could be produced anywhere, and sooner or later they were. That was the reason for the original, pre-War depression: the customers were all producing for themselves. He'd talk that over with his father. He wished he'd had time to take some economics at the University.

He found the file his father kept up-to-date on salvage sites found and registered with the Claims Office in Storisende. Some of the locations he had brought back data for had been discovered, but, to his relief, not the underground duplicate Force Command Headquarters, and not the spaceport on the island continent of Barathrum, to the east. That was all right.

He went to the house-defense arms closet and found a 10-mm Navy pistol, and a belt and spare clips. Making sure that the pistol and magazines were loaded, he buckled it on. He debated getting a vehicle out of the hangar on the landing stage, decided against it, and started downtown on foot.

29

One of the first people he met was Len Yeniguchi, the tailor. He would be at the meeting that afternoon. He managed, while talking, to comment on the cut of Conn's suit, and finger the material.

"Ah, nice," he complimented. "Made on Terra? We don't see cloth like that here very often."

He meant it wasn't Armed Forces salvage.

"Father ought to be around to see you with a bolt of material, to have a suit made," he said. "For Ghu's sake, either talk him into having a short jacket like this, or get him to buy himself a shoulder holster. He's ruined every coat he ever owned, carrying a gun on his hip."

A little farther on, he came to a combat car grounded in the middle of the street. It was green, with black trimmings, and lettered in black, GORDON VALLEY HOME GUARD. Tom Brangwyn was standing beside it, talking to a young man in a green uniform.

"Hello, Conn." The town marshal looked at his hip and grinned. "See you got all your clothes on this morning. You were just plain indecent, yesterday. . . . You know Fred Karski, don't you?"

Yes, now that Tom mentioned it, he did. He and Fred had gone to school together at the Litchfield Academy. But the six years since they'd seen each other last had made a lot of difference in both of them. He was beginning to think that the only strangers in Litchfield were his own contemporaries. They shook hands, and Conn looked at the combat car and Fred Karski's uniform.

"What's going on?" he asked. "The System States Alliance in business again?"

Karski laughed. "Oh, that's the Colonel's idea. Green and black were his colors in the War, and he's in command of the regiment."

"Regiment? You need a whole regiment?" Conn asked.

"Well, it's two companies, each about the size of a regular army platoon, but we have to call it a regiment so he can keep his old Rebel Army rank."

"We could use a regiment, Conn," Tom Brangwyn said seriously. "You have no idea how bad things have gotten.

Over on the east coast, the outlaws are looting whole towns. About four months ago, they sacked Waterville; burned the whole town and killed close to a hundred people. That was Blackie Perales' gang."

"Who is this Blackie Perales? I heard the name mentioned in connection with the *Harriet Barne*."

"Blackie Perales is anybody the Planetary Government can't catch, which means practically any outlaw," Fred Karski said.

"No, Fred; there is a Blackie Perales," Tom Brangwyn said. "He used to be a planter, down in the south. The banks foreclosed on him when he couldn't pay his notes, and he turned outlaw. That's the way it's going, all around. Every time a planter loses his plantation or a farmer loses his farm, or a mechanic loses his job, he turns outlaw. Take Tramptown, here. We used to plant nothing but melons. Then, when the sale for wine and brandy dropped, the melon-planters began cutting their melon crops and raising produce, instead of buying it from up north, and turning land into pasture for cattle. The people we used to buy foodstuffs from couldn't sell all they raised, and that threw a lot of farmhands out of work. So they got the idea there was work here, and they came flocking in, and when they couldn't get jobs, they just stayed in Tramptown, stealing anything they could. We don't even try to police Tramptown any more; we just see to it they don't come up here."

"Well, where do these outlaws and pirates who are looting whole towns come from?"

"Down in the Badlands, mostly. None of them have been bothering us, since we organized the Home Guard. They tried to, a couple of times, at first. There may have been a few survivors; they spread it around that Gordon Valley wasn't any outlaws' health resort."

"Why don't you join us, Conn?" Fred Karski asked. "All our old gang belong."

"I'd like to, but I'm afraid I'm going to be kind of busy."

Brangwyn nodded. "Yes. You will be, at that," he agreed.

"So I hear," Fred Karski said. "Do you really know where it is, Conn?"

"Well, no." He went into the routine about Merlin being still classified triple-top secret. "But we'll find it. It may take time, but we will."

They talked for a while. He asked more questions about the Home Guard. His father, it seemed, had donated all the equipment. They had a hundred and seventy men on the active list, but they had a reserve of over eight hundred, and combat vehicles and weapons on all the plantations and in all the towns along the river. The reserve had only been turned out twice; both times, outlaw attacks had been stopped dead—literally. The Home Guard, it appeared, was not given to making arrests or taking prisoners. Finally, he parted from them, strolling on along the row of stores and business places, many vacant, under the south edge of the Mall, until he saw a fluorolite sign, WADE LUCAS, M. D. He entered.

Lucas wasn't busy. They went into his consultation office, and Conn took off his gun-belt and hung it up; Lucas offered cigarettes, and they lighted and sat down.

"I see you've started carrying one," he said, nodding to the pistol Conn had laid aside.

"Civic obligation. I'm going to be too busy for Home Guard duty, but if I can protect myself, it'll save somebody else the job of protecting me."

"Maybe if there weren't so many guns around, there wouldn't be so much trouble."

He felt his good opinion of Wade Lucas start to slip. The Liberals on Terra had been full of that kind of talk, which was why only four out of ten of last year's graduating class at Armed Forces Academy had been able to get active commissions. The last war had been a disaster, so don't prepare for another one; when it comes, let it be a worse disaster.

"Guns don't make trouble; people make trouble. If the troublemakers are armed, you have to be armed too. When did you last see an Air Patrol boat around here, or even a Constabulary trooper? All we have here is the Home Guard and Tom Brangwyn and three deputies, and his pay and theirs is always six months in arrears."

THE COSMIC COMPUTER

Lucas nodded. "A bankrupt government, an unemployment rate that rises every year, currency that buys less every month. And do-it-yourself justice." The doctor blew a smoke ring and watched it float toward the ventilator-intake. "You said you're going to be busy. This company your father's talking about organizing?"

"That's right. You're going to be at the meeting at the Academy this afternoon, aren't you?"

"Yes. Just what are you going to do, after you get it organized?"

"Well, I brought back information on a great deal of undiscovered equipment and stores that the Third Force left behind. . . ." He talked on for some time, keeping to safe generalities. "It's too big for my father and me to handle alone, even if we didn't feel morally obligated to take in the people who contributed toward sending me to school on Terra. You ought to be interested in it. I know of six fully supplied hospitals, intended to take care of the casualties in case of a System States space-attack. You can imagine, better than I can, what would be in them."

"Yes. Medical supplies of all sorts are getting hard to find. But look here; you're not going to let these people waste time looking for this alleged computer, this thing they call Merlin, are you?"

"We're looking for any valuable war material. I don't know the location of Merlin, but—"

"I'll bet you don't!" Lucas said vehemently. That was the same thing Flora had said.

"—but Merlin is undoubtedly the most valuable item of abandoned TF equipment on this planet. In the long run, I'd say, more valuable than everything else together. We certainly aren't going to ignore it."

"Good heavens, Conn! You aren't like these people here; you were educated at the University of Montevideo."

"So I was. I studied computer theory and practice. I have some doubts about Merlin being able to do some of the things these laymen like Kellton and Fawzi and Judge Ledue think it could. Those sorts of misconceptions and exaggerations have to be allowed for. But I have no doubt whatever

33

that the master computer with which they did their strategic planning is probably the greatest mechanism of its sort ever built, and I have no doubt whatever that it still exists somewhere in the Alpha System."

He almost convinced himself of it. He did not, however, convince Wade Lucas, who was now regarding him with narrow-eyed suspicion.

"You mean you categorically state that that computer actually exists?"

"That, I think, was the general idea. Yes. I certainly do believe that Merlin exists."

Maybe he was telling the truth. Merlin existed in the beliefs and hopes of people like Dolf Kellton and Klem Zareff and Judge Ledue and Kurt Fawzi. Merlin was a god to them. Well, take Ghu, the Thoran Grandfather-God. Ghu was as preposterous, theologically, as Merlin was technologically; Ghu, except to Thorans, was a Federation-wide joke. But he'd known a couple of Thorans at the University, funny little fellows, with faces like terriers, their bodies covered with matted black hair. They believed in Ghu the way he believed in the Second Law of Thermodynamics. Ghu was with them every moment of their lives. Take away their belief in Ghu, and they would have been lost and wretched.

As lost and wretched as Kurt Fawzi or Judge Ledue, if they lost their belief in Merlin. He started to say something like that, and then thought better of it.

Yes, Virginia, there *is* a Santa Claus.

V

THE MEETING was at the Academy; when Conn and his father arrived, they found the central hall under the topside landing stage crowded. Kurt Fawzi and Professor Kellton had constituted themselves a reception committee. Franz Veltrin was in evidence with his audiovisual recorder, and Colonel Zareff was leaning on his silverheaded sword cane. Tom Brangwyn, in an unaccustomed best-suit. Wade Lucas, among a group of merchants, arguing heatedly.

34

Lorenzo Menardes, the distiller, and Lester Dawes, the banker, and Morgan Gatworth, the lawyer, talking to Judge Ledue. About four times as many as had been in Fawzi's office the afternoon before.

Finally, everybody was shepherded into a faculty conference room; there was a long table, and a shorter one T-wise at one end. Fawzi and Kellton conducted them to this. Both of them were trying to preside, Kellton because it was his Academy, and Fawzi ex officio as mayor and professional leading citizen, and because he had come to regard Merlin as his own private project. After everybody else was seated, the two rival chairmen-presumptive remained on their feet. Fawzi was saying, "Let's come to order; we must conduct this meeting regularly," and Kellton was saying, "Gentlemen, please; let me have your attention."

If either of them took the chair, the other would resent it. Conn got to his feet again.

"Somebody will have to preside," he said, loudly enough to cut through the babble at the long table. "Would you take the chair, Judge Ledue?"

That stopped it. Neither of them wanted to contest the honor with the president-judge of the Gordon Valley court.

"Excellent suggestion, Conn. Judge, will you preside?" Professor Kellton, who had seen himself losing out to Fawzi, asked. Fawzi threw one quick look around, estimated the situation, and got with it. "Of course, Judge. You're the logical chairman. Here, will you sit here?"

Judge Ledue took the chair, looked around for something to use as a gavel, and rapped sharply with a paperweight. "Young Mr. Conn Maxwell, who has just returned from Terra, needs no introduction to any of you," he began. Then, having established that, he took the next ten minutes to introduce Conn. When people began fidgeting, he wound up with: "Now, only about a dozen of us were at the informal meeting in Mr. Fawzi's office, yesterday. Conn, would you please repeat what you told us? Elaborate as you see fit."

Conn rose. He talked briefly about his studies on Terra to qualify himself as an expert. Then he began describing the wealth of abandoned and still undiscovered Federation

35

war material and the many installations of which he had learned, careful to avoid giving clues to exact locations. The spaceport; the underground duplicate Force Command Headquarters; the vast underground arsenals and shops and supply depots. Everybody was awed, even his father; he hadn't had time to tell him more than a fraction of it.

Finally, somebody from the long table interrupted:

"Well, Conn; how about Merlin? That's what we're interested in."

Wade Lucas snorted indignantly.

"He's telling you about real things, things worth millions of sols, and you want him to talk about that idiotic fantasy!"

There was an angry outcry. Nobody actually shouted *"To the stake with the blasphemer!"* but that was the general idea. Judge Ledue was rapping loudly for order.

"I don't know the exact location of Merlin." Conn strove to make himself heard. "The whole subject's classified top secret. But I am certain that Merlin exists, if not on Poictesme then somewhere in the Alpha System, and I am equally certain that we can find it."

Cheers. He waited for the hubbub to subside. Lucas was trying to yell above it.

"You admit you couldn't learn anything about this so-called Merlin, but you're still certain it exists?"

"Why are you certain it doesn't?"

"Why, the whole thing's absurdly fantastic!"

"Maybe it is, to a layman like you. I studied computers, and it isn't to me."

"Well, take all these elaborate preparations against space attack you were telling us about. I think Colonel Zareff, here, who served in the Alliance Army, will bear me out that such an attack was plainly impossible."

Zareff started to agree, then realized that he was aiding and comforting the enemy. "Intelligence lag," he said. "What do you expect, with General Headquarters thirty parsecs from the fighting?"

"Yes. A computer can only process the data that's been taped into it," Conn said. That was a point he wanted to ram home, as forcibly and as often as possible. "I suppose

Merlin classified an Alliance attack on Poictesme as a low-order probability, but war is the province of chance; Clausewitz said that a thousand years ago. Foxx Travis wasn't the sort of commander to let himself get caught, even by a very low-order probability."

"Well how do you explain the absence, after forty years, of any mention, in any history of the War, of Merlin? How do you get around that?"

"I don't have to. How do you get around it?"

"*Huh?*" Lucas was startled.

"Yes. Stories about Merlin were all over Poictesme, all through the Third Force, even to the enemy. Say the stories were unfounded; say Merlin never existed. Yet the belief in Merlin was an important historical fact, and no history of the War gives it so much as a footnote." He paused for effect, then continued: "That can mean only one thing. Systematic suppression, backed by the whole force of the Terran Federation. A gigantic conspiracy of silence!"

Brother! If they swallow that, I have it made; they'll swallow anything!

They did, all but Lucas. He banged his fist on the table.

"Now I've heard everything!" he shouted in disgust.

"Not quite everything, Doctor," Morgan Gatworth said. "You will hear, one of these days, that we have found Merlin."

"Yes, that'll be the day!" Lucas sprang to his feet, his chair toppling behind him. He shoved it aside with his foot. "I'm not going to argue with you. Conn Maxwell gave you a thousand-year-old quotation; I'll give you another, from Thomas Paine: 'To argue with those who have renounced the use and authority of reason is as futile as to administer medicine to the dead.' I'll add this. Conn Maxwell knows better than this balderdash he's been spouting to you. I don't know what his racket is, and I'm not staying to find out. You will, though—to your regret."

He turned and strode from the room. There was a moment's silence, after the door slammed behind him. Too bad, Conn thought. He would have made a good friend. Now he was going to make a very nasty enemy.

"Well, let's get to business," his father said. "We don't have to argue about the existence of Merlin; we know that. Let's discuss the question of finding it."

"I still think it's somewhere off-planet," Lorenzo Menardes said. "The moons of Pantagruel . . ."

Evidently he'd read something, or seen an old film, about the moons of Pantagruel.

"No, that's too far; they'd keep it where they could use it."

"The old GHQ," Lester Dawes suggested. "Suppose it's down under that, like the place Rodney found under Tenth Army."

"I hope not," Gathworth said. "The Planetary Government took that over."

"Well, wherever it is, finding it is going to be expensive," Rodney Maxwell said. "Now, to finance the search, I propose we use this information my son brought back from Terra. Doctor Lucas was right about one thing; that's worth millions of sols. Well, I propose, also, that we set up a company and get it chartered; a prospecting company, to operate under the Abandoned Property Act of 867. My son and I will contribute this information as our share in the capitalization of the company. The work of opening these Federation installations can go on concurrently with the search for Merlin, and the profits can finance it."

Silence for a moment, then a bedlam of cheering.

"Well, let's get organized," Gathworth said. "What will we call this company?"

A number of voices shouted suggestions. Rodney Maxwell managed to get recognition and partial silence.

"It is of the first importance," he said, "that we keep our real objective—Merlin—as close a secret as possible. The Planetary Government would like to get hold of it—and I leave you to ask yourselves how far Jake Vyckhoven and his cronies are to be trusted with anything like that—and I have no doubt the Federation might try to take it away from us."

"Couldn't do it, Rodney," Judge Ledue objected. "Everything the Federation abandoned in the Trisystem is public domain now. We have a Federation Supreme Court ruling—"

"What's legality to the Federation?" Klem Zareff demanded. "They fought a criminally illegal war of aggression against my people."

Down the table, somebody started singing "Rally Round the Banner, the Banner Black and Green."

"Well, I think it's a good idea to keep quiet about it, myself," Kurt Fawzi said.

"All right," Rodney Maxwell said. "Then we don't want this company to sound like anything but another salvage company. I suggest we call it Litchfield Exploration & Salvage."

"Good name, Rodney," Dawes approved. "That a motion? I second it."

Unanimously carried. They had a name, now, anyhow. Everybody began suggesting other topics for consideration—capitalization, application for charter, election of officers, stock issues. Conn paid less and less attention. Industrial finance and organization wasn't his subject, either. His father was plunging happily into it as though he had been promoting companies all his life. Conn sat and doodled with his six-color pen, mostly spherical hyperspace ships.

"We can't get all this cleared up now," Lester Dawes was protesting. "Your Honor, I mean, Mr. Chairman; I suggest that committees be appointed. . . ."

More hassling; everybody wanted to be on all the committees. Finally, they appointed enough committees to include everybody.

"Well, that seems to be cleared up," Judge Ledue said. "I suggest a meeting day after tomorrow evening; the committees should have everything set up, and we should be able to organize ourselves and elect permanent officers. Is there anything else to discuss, or do I hear a motion to adjourn?"

Somebody thought they ought to have some idea of what the first operation would be.

"You heard me mention a spaceport," Conn said. "I can tell you, now, that it's over on Barathrum, inside the crater of an extinct volcano. I think we ought to have a look at that, first of all."

"I know you seemed to think yesterday that Merlin is off-planet," Fawzi said. "I'm inclined to disagree, Conn. I think it's right here on Poictesme."

"We ought to nail that spaceport down first," Conn argued.

"Conn, you mentioned an underground duplicate of Travis's general headquarters," Zareff said. "They thought we'd possibly send a fleet here to blitz Poictesme, or they wouldn't have built that. And this underground headquarters would be the safest place on the planet; they'd make sure of that. Staff brass don't like to get caught out in the rain, not when it's raining hellburners and planetbusters. Merlin would be too big to take there along with them, so they'd put it there in the first place."

That made sense. If he'd been Foxx Travis, and if there had been a Merlin, that was exactly where he'd have put it himself. But there was no Merlin, and he wanted a ship. He argued mulishly for a little, then saw that it was hopeless and gave in.

"I want to find Merlin as much as any of you," he said. "More. Merlin was the only thing I was trained for. We'll look there first."

Somebody asked where, approximately, this underground Force Command headquarters was.

"Why, it's in the Badlands, over between the Blaubergs and the east coast."

"Great Ghu! We'll need an army to go in there?" Tom Brangwyn said. "That's where all these outlaws have been coming from, Blackie Perales and all."

"Then we'll get an army together," Klem Zareff said happily. "Might make a little of that reward money that's been offered."

"We'll need more than that. We'll need excavation equipment, and labor. Lots of labor," Conn said. "It's a couple of hundred feet below the surface; from the plans, I'd say they just dug a big pit, built the headquarters in it, and filled it in. There are two entrances, a vertical shaft and a horizontal tunnel."

"When they pulled out, they probably filled the shaft and

40

vitrified the rock at the outer ends," his father added. "That was what they did at Tenth Army."

Another idea hit him. "Mr. Mayor, do you think you could set up some kind of a public-works program here in Litchfield? We can't start this till after the wine-pressing's over, and we'll need a lot of labor, as I pointed out. Now, it's important that we keep all our projects a secret until we can get our claims filed. If we start this municipal fix-up-and-clean-up program, we can give work to a lot of these drifters who haven't been able to get jobs on the plantations, get them organized into gangs, and keep them together till we're ready for the Force Command job."

Lorenzo Menardes supported the idea. "And while they were boondoggling around in Litchfield, we could pick out the best workers, get rid of the incompetents, and train a few supervisors. That's going to be one of our worst headaches; getting capable supervisors."

"You telling me?" Rodney Maxwell asked. "That was what I was wondering about: where we'd get gang-bosses. And another thing; this municipal housecleaning would mask our real preparations."

"Well, we need something like that," Fawzi said. "We've needed it for a long time. I guess it took Conn, coming home from Terra, to see how badly we've let the town get run down. Franz, suppose you and Tom Brangwyn and Lorenzo form a committee on that. Look around, see what needs fixing up worst, and set up a project. Who's city engineer now?"

"Abe O'Leary; he died six years ago," Dawes said. "You never appointed his successor."

"Well, I guess I never got around to that," the mayor of Litchfield admitted.

When the meeting finally adjourned, they went up and got in the car; his father lifted it straight up to thirty thousand feet and started circling. An aircar was one place where they could talk safely.

"Conn, I was kind of worried, down there. You were being a little too positive. You know, you're only twenty-three. As long as you agree with those people, you're a brilliant

41

young man; you start getting ideas of your own, and you're just a half-baked kid. You let the older and wiser heads run things. You can't begin to hope to foul things up the way they can. Look at all the experience they've had."

"But we've got to have a ship. Everything depends on that."

"I know it does. We'll get a ship. Let Kurt Fawzi and Klem Zareff and the rest of them have this duplicate Force Command thing first, though. Keep them happy. As soon as we have that opened, you can take a gang and run over to Barathrum and grab your spaceport. Wait till they find out that Merlin isn't at Force Command Duplicate. Then you can convince them it's really on Koshchei."

VI

THE CAR Rodney Maxwell got out of the hangar the next morning wasn't the one he and Conn had gone to the meeting in; it was the one he had flown in from Tenth Army HQ at noon of the previous day. An Army reconnaissance job, slim and needlelike, completely enclosed, looking more like a missile than a vehicle, and armored in dazzling, iridescent collapsium. There was something to living on Poictesme, at that; only a millionaire on Terra could have owned a car like that.

"Nice," Conn said. "Where did you dig it?"

"Where we're going, Tenth Army."

"I'll bet she'll do Mach Three."

"Better than that. I've never had her above 2.5, but the airspeed gauge is marked up to four. And she has everything: all kinds of detection instruments, cameras, audio-visual pickups, armament. And the armor; you can take her through any kind of radiation."

The armor was only a couple of micromicrons thick, but it would stop anything. It was collapsed matter, the electron shells of the atoms collapsed upon the nuclei, the atoms in actual contact. That plating made eighth-inch sheet steel as heavy as twelve-inch armor plate, and in texture and shielding properties, lead was like sponge by comparison.

They climbed in, and Rodney Maxwell snapped on the
screens that served as windows. Conn leaned back and
looked at the underside view in a screen on the roof of the
car, as his father started the lift-engine.

"Still think it's worth the price, son?" his father asked.

The price had begun to rise; even so, he was afraid that
what they had paid so far was only the down payment.
Dinner last evening. Flora, who had evidently been talking
to Wade Lucas, shouting accusations at them; his mother
fleeing from the table in tears. As the car rose, he reached
out and turned on and adjusted the telescreen for the under-
view.

"Keep your eye on that, Father," he said. "That's what
we're paying to get rid of."

A distillery, bigger than the Menardes plant, long closed
and now half roofless and crumbling. Rows of warehouses,
empty after the War until taken over by homeless vagrants.
Jerry-built shanties with rattletrap aircars grounded around
them. Tramptown, a festering sore on the south side of
Litchfield.

"If we put this over," he continued, "all those tramps will
have steady work and good homes. We can have a park
there, with fountains that'll work. Maybe even Flora and
Mother will think we've done something worth doing."

"It'll be kind of hard to take in the meantime, though, but
if you can take it, I can." Rodney Maxwell turned off the
underside teleview screen and put on the forward one. "See
that little pink spot over there? Sunrise on the east side of
Snagtooth; Tenth Army's just behind us. Now, let's see if
this airspeed gauge is telling the truth or just bragging."

Sudden acceleration pushed them back in their seats. The
calibrations on the gauge rose swiftly; the pink-lighted peak
grew swiftly in the teleview screen. The gauge hadn't been
bragging, it had been understating; the car had more speed
than the instrument could register. Two and a half minutes
from Litchfield, they were decelerating and swinging
slowly around Snagtooth, looking down on a tilted plateau
that ended on the western side in a sheer drop of almost
a thousand feet.

There were ruinous buildings on it: barracks and store-houses and offices, an airship dock and an air-traffic control tower from which all the glass had long ago vanished, a great steel telecast tower that had fallen, crushing a couple of buildings. Young trees had already grown among the wreckage.

"Look over there, on the slope below it; there's one entrance to the shelters." There was a clearing among the evergreens, half a mile from the buildings, and raw earth, and a couple of big scows grounded near. "They bulldozed rock and earth over the end of the tunnel. Then, there's another one down on that bench, a couple of hundred feet below the edge of the plateau. They blasted rock down over that. The main entrance is a vertical shaft under that pre-stressed concrete dome. That was chapel, auditorium, or something. They just covered it with sheet metal and poured a foot of concrete on top."

They floated down above the broken roofs and crumbling walls, and grounded in the area between the main administration building and the offices, back of the ship docks. Once, he supposed, it had been a lawn. Then it had been a jungle. Now it was a scuffed, littered, bare-trodden workyard. Men were straggling out of the administration building, lighting pipes and cigarettes; they all wore new but work-soiled infantry battle dress. All of them waved and shouted greetings; one, about Conn's own age, approached. As he got out, Conn saw the resemblance to Lester Dawes, the banker, before he recognized Anse Dawes, who had been one of his closest friends six years ago. They shook hands and pounded each other on the back.

"Hey, you're looking great, Conn!" They all told him that; he'd begin to believe it pretty soon. "Sorry I couldn't make the party, but somebody had to sit on the lid here, and Jerry Rivas and I cut cards for it and Jerry won."

"You didn't tell me Anse was with you," he reproached his father. Rodney Maxwell said he'd been saving that for a surprise.

When Conn asked Anse what was the matter with the bank, he said: "For the birds; I'd as soon count sheets of

44

toilet paper as this stuff we're using for money. Sooner. Toilet paper can be used for something, and this paper money's too stiff. Maybe some of this stuff we're digging here isn't worth much, but at least it's real."

That was something else the Maxwell Plan would have to take care of. Gresham's Law was running hog-wild on Poictesme. A Planetary Government sol was worth about ten centisols, Federation, and aside from deposit boxes, woolen socks under the mattress, and tin cans buried in the corner of the cellar, Federation currency was nonexistent.

"Had breakfast yet?" Rodney Maxwell asked.

"Oh, hours ago. I was out and shot another spikenose; it's hanging up back of the kitchen, waiting for the cook to skin it and cut it up." He grinned at Conn. "You don't get this kind of hunting in a bank, either."

"Jerry still inside? I want to see him. Suppose you take Conn around and show him the sights. And don't worry about him bumping you out of a job. Worry about the six or eight extra jobs you'll have to do besides your own, from now on."

Conn and Anse crossed the yard and entered one of the office buildings, through a big breach in the wall. Anse said: "I did that myself; 90-mm tank gun. When we want a wall out of the way, we get it out of the way." Inside were a lot of lifters and skids and power shovels and things; laborers were assembling for work assignments. Most of them had been with his father six years ago and he knew them. They hadn't done any growing up in the meantime. They climbed into an airjeep and floated out over the edge of the plateau, letting down past the sheer cliff to where the lower lateral shaft had been opened. A great deal of rock had been shoveled and bulldozed away to expose it; it was twenty feet high and forty wide. Anse simply steered the jeep inside and up the tunnel.

There were occasional lights on at the ceiling. Anse said they were all powered from their own nuclear-electric conversion units. "We don't have the central power on here; there's a big mass-energy converter, but we're tearing it down to ship out."

That was something they could get a good price for. Maybe even one-tenth of what it was worth. At least they wouldn't have to sell it by the ton.

The tunnel ended in an enormous room a couple of hundred feet square and fifty high. There was a wide aisle up the middle; on either side, contragravity equipment was massed. Tanks with long 90-mm guns. Combat cars. Small airboats. Rank on rank of air-cavalry single-mounts, egg-shaped things just big enough for a man to sit in, with quadruple machine guns in front and flame-jets behind. Ambulances armored against radiation; decontamination units; mobile workshops; mobile kitchens. Troop carriers, jeeps, staff cars; power shovels, manipulators, lifters. All waiting, for forty years, to swarm out as soon as the bombs that never came stopped falling.

They floated the jeep along hallways beyond, and got down to look into rooms. Work was already going on in the power plant; a gang under a slim young man whom Anse introduced as Mohammed Matsui were using repair-robots to get canisters of live plutonium out of a reactor. Workshops. Laundries. Storerooms. Kitchens, some stripped and a few still intact. A hospital. Guardhouse and lockup.

More storerooms on the level above, reached by returning to the vehicle hangar and lifting to an upper entrance. By this time, gangs were at work there, too, moving contragravity skids in empty and out loaded.

"The CO here must have had squirrel blood," Anse said. "I think when the evacuation orders came through he just gathered up everything there was topside and crammed it down here, any old way. Honest to Ghu, this place was packed solid when we found it. Nobody'd believe it."

"Wait till you see the next one."

"You mean there's another place like this?"

"You can say so. You can say a twenty-megaton thermonuclear is like a hand grenade, too."

Anse Dawes simply didn't believe that.

When they got back to the Administration Building on top, they found Rodney Maxwell, Jerry Rivas, the general foremen, and half a dozen gang foremen, in consultation.

46

THE COSMIC COMPUTER

"We're getting a hundred and fifty more men and ten farm scows from Litchfield," his father said. "Dave McCade's coming out from our yard, and Tom Brangwyn's sending one of his deputies to help boss them. We'll have to keep an eye on this crowd; they're all Tramptown hoodlums, but that's the best we can get. We're going to have to get this place cleaned out in a hurry. We only have about two weeks till the wine-pressing's over, and then we want to start the next operation. Conn, did you see all that engineering equipment, down on the bottom level?"

"Yes. I think we ought to leave a lot of that here—the shovels and bulldozers and manipulators and so on. We can move it direct to Force Command. How are we fixed for blasting explosives?"

"Name it and we have it. Cataclysmite, FJ-7, anything you want."

"We'll need a lot of it."

"We're going to have to get a ship. I mean a contragravity ship, a freighter; first, to move this stuff out of here, and then to move the stuff out of Force Command. And we want it mounted with heavy armament, too. We not only want a freighter, we want a fighting ship."

"You think so?"

"I'm sure of it," Rodney Maxwell said. "Where we're going is full of outlaws; there must be hundreds of them holing up over there. That's where all the trouble on the east coast comes from. Now, outlaws are sure-thing players. They want to be alive to spend their loot, and they won't tackle anything that's too tough for them. A lot of guards and combat equipment may look like a loss on the books, but the books won't show how much of a loss you might take if you didn't have them. I want this operation armed till it'll be too much for all the outlaws on the planet to tackle."

That made sense. It also made sense out of the billions of sols the Federation had spent preparing for an invasion that never came. If it had come and found them unprepared, the loss might have been the war itself.

The scows and the newly hired workers began arriving a little after noon. The scows had been borrowed from plantations where the crop had been gotten in; there were melon leaves and bits of vine in the bottoms. The workers were a bleary-eyed and unsavory lot; Conn had a suspicion, which Brangwyn's deputy confirmed, that they had been collected by mass vagrancy arrests in Tramptown. As soon as they started arriving, Jerry Rivas hurried down to the old provost-marshal's headquarters and came back with a lot of rubber billy-clubs, which he issued to his gang-bosses, regular and temporary. A few times they had to be used. By evening, however, the insubordinate and troublesome had been quieted. They would all steal anything they could put in their pockets, but that was to be expected. By evening, too, the contents of the underground treasure trove was moving out in a steady stream, and scows were shuttling to and from Litchfield.

Rodney Maxwell was going back to town after lunch the next day. Conn wanted to know if he should go along.

"No, you stay here; help keep things moving. Remember what I told you about the older and wiser heads? Let me handle them. I've been around them, heaven pity me, longer than you have. Just give me an audiovisual of your proxy and I'll vote your stock."

"How much stock do I have, by the way?"

"The same as I have—ten thousand five hundred shares of common, at twenty centisols a share. But watch where it goes after we open Force Command."

His father was back, two days later, to report:

"We're organized. Kurt Fawzi's president, of course, and does he love it. That'll keep him out of mischief. Dolf Kellton's secretary; he has an office force at the Academy and can conscript students to help. He's organizing a research team from his seniors and post-grad students to work in the Planetary Library at Storisende. There are a lot of old Third Force records there; he may find something useful. Of course, Lester Dawes is treasurer."

"What are you?"

"Vice-president in charge of operations. That's what I

spent all yesterday log-rolling, baby-kissing and cigar-passing to get."

"And what am I, if it's a fair question?"

"You have a very distinguished position; you are a non-office-holding stockholder. The only other one is Judge Ledue; as a member of the judiciary, he did not feel it proper to accept official position in a private corporation. Tom Brangwyn's Chief of Company Police; Klem Fawzi is Commander of the Company Guards. And we have a law firm in Storisende lined up to handle our charter application. Sterber, Flynn & Chen-Wong. Sterber's married to Jake Vyckhoven's sister, Flynn's son is married to the daughter of the Secretary of the Treasury, and Chen-Wong is a nephew of the Chief Justice. All of them are directly descended from members of Genji Gartner's original crew."

"You don't anticipate any trouble about getting the charter?"

"Not exactly. And Lester Dawes is in Storisende now, trying to find us a contragravity ship. There are about a dozen in the hands of receivers for bankrupt shipping companies; he might find one that's still airworthy. Oh; you remember how I insisted on absolute secrecy about our Merlin objective? That's working out better than my fondest expectations. It's leaking like a machine-gunned water tank, and everybody it leaks to is positive that we know exactly where Merlin is or we wouldn't be trying to keep it a secret."

Three days later, Conn hitched a ride on a freight-scow to Litchfield. From the air, he could see a haze of bonfire smoke over High Garden Terrace, and a gang of men at work. There were more men at work on the Mall and along the streets on either side. He went up from the yard below the house, where the scow was being unloaded, and found his mother in the living room watching a screen play with one eye and keeping the other on a soulless machine like a miniature contragravity tank, which was going over the carpet with a vacuum cleaner and taking swipes at the furniture with a rotary dustmop. She was glad to see him, and then became troubled.

49

"Conn, when Flora comes home, you won't argue with her, will you?"

"Only in self-defense." That was the wrong thing to say. He changed it to, "No; I won't argue with her at all," and then quoted Wade Lucas quoting Thomas Paine. Then he had to assure his mother a couple of times that there really was a Merlin, and then assure her that it wouldn't get loose and hurt anybody if he did find it.

In the middle of his assurances about the harmlessness of Merlin, the housecleaning-robot began knocking things off the top of a table.

"Oscar! You stop that!" his mother yelled.

Oscar, deaf as the adder, kept on. Conn yelled at his mother to use her control; she remembered that she had one, a thing like an old-fashioned pocket watch, around her neck on a chain, and got the robot stopped.

No wonder she was afraid of Merlin.

He took advantage of the interruption to get to his room and change clothes, then went up to the hangar and got out an air-cavalry mount. About fifty men were working on High Garden Terrace, pruning and trimming and leveling the lawns. There was a big vitrifier on the Mall—even at five hundred feet he could feel the heat from it—chuffing and clanking and pouring lavalike molten rock for a new pavement. And all the nymphs and satyrs and dryads and fauns and centaurs had had their pedestals rebuilt and were sandblasted clean.

He landed on the top of the Airlines Building and rode a lift down to the office where Kurt Fawzi neglected the affairs of his shipline agency, his brokerage business, and the city of Litchfield. The afternoon habitués had begun to gather— Raymond Fitch, the used-vehicles dealer, Lorenzo Menardes, Judge Ledue, Tom Brangwyn, Klem Zareff. Fawzi was on the screen, talking to somebody with sandy hair and a suit that didn't seem to be made of any sort of Federation Armed Forces material, about warehouse facilities. The addresses they were mentioning were in Storisende.

"No, Leo, I don't know when," Fawzi was saying, "but don't you worry. You just have space for it, and we'll fill it up.

And don't ask me what sort of stuff. You know what a salvage operation's like; you just haul out the stuff as you come to it."

Tom Brangwyn, lounging in one of the deep chairs, looked up.

"Hello, Conn. We're having a time. Another two hundred tramps came in on the *Countess* this morning, and Ghu only knows how many in their own vehicles, and they all seem to think if there's work for some there ought to be work for all, and some of them are getting nasty."

"We can use some more out at the dig. The ones you sent out Thursday are doing all right, once they found out we weren't taking any foolishness."

Fawzi turned away from the screen. "Well, Conn, we're in," he said. "The charter was granted this morning; now we're Litchfield Exploration & Salvage, Ltd. And Lester Dawes has found us a contragravity ship."

"How much will it cost us?"

Fawzi began to laugh. "Conn, this'll slay you! She isn't costing us a centisol. You know those old ships on Mothball Row, back of the old West End ship docks at Storisende?"

Conn nodded. He'd seen them before he had gone away, and from the *City of Asgard* coming in—a lot of old Army Transport craft, covered with muslin and sprayed with protectoplast. The Planetary Government had taken them over after the War and forgotten them.

"Well, Lester's getting one of them for us under the old 878 Commercial Enterprise Encouragement Act. She's an Army combat freighter, regimental ammunition ship. Of course, she still has armament; we'll have to pay to get that off."

"Why?"

Fawzi looked at him in surprise. "It would only be in the way and add weight. We want her for a cargo ship, don't we?"

"That's what she was built for. What kind of armament?"

Fawzi didn't know. Klem Zareff did.

"Four 115-mm rifles, two fore and two aft. A pair of lift-and-drive missile launchers amidships. And a secondary gun

51

battery of 70-mm's and 50-mm auto-cannon. I know the class; we captured a few of them. Good ships."

Fawzi was horrified. "Why, that's more firepower than the whole Air Patrol. Look, the Government won't like our having anything like that."

"They're giving her to us, aren't they?" Menardes asked.

"Gehenna with what the Government likes!" the old Rebel swore. "If they'd put a few of those ships into commission, they could wipe out these outlaws and a private company wouldn't need an armed ship."

"May I use your screen, Kurt?" Conn asked.

When Fawzi nodded, he punched out the combination of the operating office at Tenth Army, and finally got his father on. He told him about the ship.

"There's talk about tearing the armament out," he added.

"Is that so, now? Well, I'll call Lester Dawes before he can get started on it. I think I'll go in to Storisende tomorrow and see the ship for myself. See what I can do about ammunition for those guns, too."

"But, Rod," Fawzi protested, joining the conversation, "we don't want to start a war."

"No. We want to stay out of one. You don't do that by disarming. We're taking that ship down into the Badlands. Remember?" Rodney Maxwell said. "Ever hear the name Blackie Perales?"

Fawzi had. He stopped arguing about armament. Instead, he began worrying about how much the civic clean-up campaign was costing Litchfield.

"You think we really need that, Rod?"

"Of course we do. You'd be surprised how much labor we're going to need, and how hard up we're going to be for capable supervisors. This thing's a training program, Kurt, and we'll need every man we train on it."

"But it's costing like Nifflheim, Rod. We're going to bankrupt the city."

"Worse than it is now, you mean? Oh, don't worry, Kurt. As soon as we find Merlin, everything'll be all right."

Franz Veltrin came in, shortly after Rodney Maxwell was off the screen. He dropped his audiovisual camera and sound recorder on the table, laid his pistol-belt on top of them and took a drink of brandy, downing it with the audible satisfaction of a thirsty horse at a trough. Then he looked around accusingly.

"Somebody's been talking!" he declared. "I've had all the news services on the planet on my screen today; they all want the story about what's happening here. They've heard we know where Merlin is; that Conn Maxwell found out on Terra."

"They just put two and two together and threw seven," Conn said. "A *Herald-Guardian* ship-news reporter interviewed me when I got in, and found out I'd been studying cybernetics and computer theory on Terra. What did you tell them?"

"Complete denial. We don't know a thing about Merlin. Naturally, they didn't believe me. A bunch of them are coming out here tomorrow. What are we going to tell them? We'll all have to have the same story."

"I," said Judge Ledue, "am not going to be interviewed, I am leaving town till they're gone."

"Why don't you steer them onto Wade Lucas?" Conn asked. "If you want anything denied, he'll do it for you."

Everybody thought that was a wonderful idea, except Klem Zareff, and he waited until Conn was ready to go and rode up to the landing stage with him.

"Conn, I know this Lucas is going to marry your sister," he began, "but how much do you know about him?"

"Not much. He seems like a nice chap. I don't hold what he said at the meeting against him. I suppose if I'd come from off-planet, I wouldn't believe in Merlin either."

"Hah! But doesn't he believe in Merlin?"

"He makes noises like it."

"You know what I think?" Klem Zareff lowered his voice to a whisper. "I think he's a Federation spy! I think the Federation's lost Merlin. That's why they haven't come back to get it long ago."

"Pretty big thing to mislay."

"It could happen. There'd only be a few scientists and some high staff officers who'd know where it was. Well, say

53

they all went back to Terra on the same ship, and the ship was lost at space. Sabotage, one of our commerce raiders that hadn't heard the War was over, maybe just an ordinary accident. But the ship's lost, and the location of Merlin's lost with her."

"That could happen," Conn agreed seriously.

"All right. So ever since, they've had people here, listening, watching, spying. This Lucas; he showed up here about a year after you went to Terra. And who does he get engaged to? Your sister. And what does he do here? Goes around arguing that there is no Merlin, getting people to argue with him, getting them mad, so they'll blurt out anything they know. I'm an old field officer; I know all the prisoner-interrogation tricks in the book, and that's always been one of the best."

"Then why did he act the way he did at the meeting? All he did there was cut himself off from learning anything more from any of us. In his place, would you have done that? No; you'd have tried to take the lead in hunting for Merlin yourself. Now wouldn't you?"

Zareff was silent, first puzzled, and then hurt. Now he would have to tear the whole idea down and build it over.

Flora was quite friendly when she came home from school. She'd found out, somewhere, that Conn had been the originator of the municipal face-lifting project. He was tempted, briefly, to tell her a little, if not all, of the truth about the Maxwell Plan, then decided against it. The way to keep a secret was to confide it to nobody; every time you did, you doubled, maybe even squared, the chances of exposure.

He told his father, when Rodney Maxwell came in from the dig, about his talk with Klem Zareff.

"How long's he been like that, anyhow?" he asked.

"As long as I've known him. When it comes to melons and wine and bossing tramp labor and taking care of his money and coming in out of the rain, Klem Zareff's as sane as I am. But on the subject of the Terran Federation, he's crazy as a bedbug. What is a bedbug, anyhow?"

"They have them on Terra, in places like Tramptown. They have places like Tramptown on Terra, too."

"Uhuh. I suppose, in Klem's boots, I'd be just as crazy as he is," Rodney Maxwell said. "One minute, he had a wife and two children in Kindelburg, on Ashmodai, and the next minute Kindelburg was a puddle of radioactive slag."

"That was in '51, wasn't it? I read about it," Conn said. "It was a famous victory."

That was from a poem, too.

Rodney Maxwell flew to Storisende early the next morning. Conn rode back to Tenth Army on an empty scow and pitched into the job of getting the stores and equipment out of the underground shelters. More farm-tramps arrived, and had to be pounded into obedience and taught the work. At the same time, Litchfield was getting a steady influx of job-seekers, and a secondary swarm of thugs, grifters and gangsters who followed them. Klem Zareff, having gotten all his melons pressed, came out to Tenth Army, where he selected fifty of the best men from the work-gangs and began drilling them as soldiers to guard the next operation. The manual of arms, drill and salute he taught them was, of course, System States Alliance.

A week later, the ship arrived from Storisende; a hundred and sixty feet, three thousand tons, small enough to be berthed inside a hyperspace transport, and fast enough to get a load of ammunition to troops at the front, unload, and get out again before the enemy could zero in on her, and armed to fight off any Army Air Force combat craft. The delay had been in recruiting officers and crew. The captain and chief engineer were out-of-work shipline officers, the gunner was a former Federation artillery officer, and the crew looked more like pirates than most pirates did.

They christened her the *Lester Dawes*, because Dawes had secured her and because the name began with the initials of Litchfield Exploration & Salvage. From then on, it was a race to see whether the Tenth Army attack-shelters would be emptied before the wine was all pressed, or vice versa.

VII

FIFTY-TWO years before, they had come to the mesa in the Badlands and dug a pit on top of it, a thousand feet in diameter and more than five hundred deep, and in it they built a duplicate of the headquarters for Third Fleet-Army Force Command. They built a shaft a hundred feet in diameter like a chimney at one side, and they ran a tunnel out through solid rock to the head of a canyon half a mile away. Then they buried the whole thing. Twelve years later, when the War was over, they sealed both entrances and went away and left it.

For a month each winter, cold rains from the east lashed the desert; for the rest of the year, it was swept by wind-blown sand. Wiregrass sprouted, and thornbush grew; Nature, the master-camoufleur, completed the work of hiding the forgotten headquarters. Little things not unlike rabbits scampered over it, and bigger things, vaguely foxlike, hunted them. Hunted men came, too, their aircars skimming low. None of them had the least idea what was underneath.

The mesa-top came suddenly to life, just as the sun edged up out of the east. Conn and his father and Anse Dawes came in first, in the recon-car with which they had scouted and photographed the site a few days before. They circled at a thousand feet, fired a smoke bomb, and then let down near where Conn's map showed the head of the vertical shaft. The rest followed, first a couple of combat cars that circled slowly, scanning the ground, and then the *Lester Dawes* with her big guns and her load of equipment, and behind a queue of boats and scows and heavy engineering equipment on con-tragravity and troop carriers full of workmen and guards, flanked by air cavalry, which circled above while everything else landed, then scattered out over a fifty-mile radius. Occasionally there was a hammering of machine guns, either because somebody saw something on the ground that might need shooting at or simply because it was a beautiful morning to make a noise.

The ship settled quickly and daintily, while Conn and Anse and Rodney Maxwell sat in the car and watched. Immediately, she began opening like a beetle bursting from its shell, large sections of armor swinging outward. Except for the bridge and the gun turrets, almost the whole ship could be opened; she had been designed to land in the middle of a battle and deliver ammunition when seconds could mean the difference between life and death. Jeeps and lifters and manipulators and things floated out of her. Scows began landing and unloading prefab-hut elements. A water tank landed, and the cook-shed began going up beside it; a lorry came in with scanning and probing equipment, and a couple of men jumped off and huddled over a photoprint copy of one of Conn's maps.

Conn lifted the car again and coasted it half a mile to where the cleft in the mesa started. There were half a dozen claw-armed manipulators already there, and two giant power shovels. Jerry Rivas and one of the engineers Kurt Fawzi had hired had gotten out of a jeep and were looking at another photoprint of the map. Rivas pointed to the head of the canyon, where a mass of rock had slid down.

"That's it; you can still see where they put off the shots."

The canyon was long enough and wide enough for the *Lester Dawes* to land in it; she could be loaded directly from the tunnel. The manipulators began moving in, wrestling with the larger chunks of rock and dragging or carrying them away. Power shovels began grunting and clanking and rumbling; dust rose in a thick column. Toward midmorning, the troop carriers which served as school buses in Litchfield arrived, loaded with more workmen. A lorry lettered STOR-ISENDE HERALD-GUARDIAN came in, hovered over the canyon, and began transmitting audiovisuals. More news-folk put in an appearance.

The earth and rock at the top of the tunnel entrance fell

57

away, revealing the vitrified stone lintel; everybody cheered and dug harder. More aircars arrived, getting in each other's and everybody else's way. Raymond Fitch, Lester Dawes, Lorenzo Menardes and Morgan Gatworth. Dolf Kellton, playing hookey from school. Kurt Fawzi; he landed in the canyon and watched every shovelful of rock lifted, as though trying to help with mental force. Tom Brangwyn, with a score of the Home Guard to reinforce the Company Police. Klem Zareff called in his air cavalry to help control the sightseers. Nobody was making trouble; they were just getting in the way.

At eleven, Rodney Maxwell went aboard the *Lester Dawes* to use the radio and telescreen equipment. By then, two time zones west in Storisende, the Claims Office was opening; he filed preliminary claim to an underground installation with at least two entrances in uninhabited country, and claimed a ten-mile radius around it. By that time, the gang working on top had uncovered a virtrified slab over the hundred-foot circle of the vertical shaft and were cracking it with explosives. According to the scanners, it was full of loose rubble for a hundred feet down. Below that, the microrays hit something impenetrable.

Toward midafternoon, the tunnel in the canyon was cleared. It had been vitrified solid; the scanners reported that it was plugged for ten feet. A contragravity tank let down in front of it, with a solenoid jackhammer mounted where the gun should have been, and began pounding, running a hole in for a blast shot. There were more explosions topside; when Conn took a jeep up to observe progress there, he found the vitrified rock blown completely off the vertical shaft, exposing the rubble that had been dumped into it. The gang on the mesa-top had discovered something else; a grid of auro-copper bussbars buried four feet underground. Ten to one, radio and telescreen signals would be transmitted to that from below, and then probably picked up and rebroadcast from a relay station on one or another of the high buttes in the neighborhood. Time enough to look for that later. He returned to the canyon, where the lateral tunnel was now almost completely open.

When it was clear, they sent a snooper in first. It was a robot, looking slightly like a short-tailed tadpole, six feet long by three feet at the thickest. It transmitted a view of the tunnel as it went slowly in; the air, it found, was breathable, and there were no harmful radiations or other dangers. According to the plans, there should be a big room at the other end, slightly curved, a hundred feet wide by a hundred on either side of the tunnel entrance. The robot entered this, and in its headlight they could see reconnaissance-cars, and contragravity tanks with 90-mm guns. It swerved slightly to the left, and then the screen stopped receiving, the telemetered instruments went dead and the robot's signal stopped.

"Tom," Rodney Maxwell said, "you keep the crowd back. Klem, stay with the screens; I'll transmit to you. I'm going in to see what's wrong."

He started to give Conn an argument when he wanted to accompany him.

"No," Conn said. "I'm going along. What do you think I went to Terra to study robotics for?"

His father snapped on the screen and pickup of the jeep that was standing nearby. "You getting it, Klem?" he asked. "Okay, Conn. Let's go."

Half a mile ahead, at the other end of the tunnel, they could see a flicker of light that grew brighter as they advanced. The snooper still had its light on and was moving about. Once they caught a momentary signal from it. As Rodney Maxwell piloted the jeep, Conn kept talking to Klem Zareff, outside. Then they were at the end of the tunnel and entering the room ahead; it was full of vehicles, like the one on the bottom level at Tenth Army HQ. As soon as they were inside, Klem Zareff's voice in the radio stopped, as though the set had been shot out.

"Klem! What's wrong? We aren't getting you," his father was saying.

The snooper was drifting aimlessly about, avoiding the parked vehicles. Conn used the manual control to set it down and deactivate it, then got out and went to examine it.

"Take the jeep over to the tunnel entrance," he told his

father. "Move out into the tunnel a few feet; relay from me to Klem."

The jeep moved over. A moment later his father cried, "He's getting me; I'm getting him. What's the matter with the radio in here? The snooper's all right, isn't it?"

It was. Conn reactivated it and put it up above the tops of the vehicles.

"Sure. We just can't transmit out."

"But only half a mile of rock; that set's good for more than that. It'll transmit clear through Snagtooth."

"It won't transmit through collapsium."

His father swore disgustedly, repeating it to Zareff outside. Conn could hear the old soldier, in the radio, make a smiliar remark. They should have all expected that, in the first place. If the Third Force High Command was expecting to sit out a nuclear bombardment in this place, they'd armor it against anything.

"Bring the gang in; it's safe as far as we've gotten," his father said. "We'll just have to string wires out."

Conn used his flashlight and found the power unit for the room lights; all the overhead lights were wired to one unit, if wired were the word for gold-leaf circuits cemented to the walls and covered with insulating paint. For the heavy stuff, like the ventilator fans, they'd have to find the central power plant. He looked around the big room, poking into some of the closets that lined it. Radiation-proof clothing. Tools. Arms and ammunition. First-aid kits. Emergency rations. All the vehicles were plated in shimmering collapsium.

The crowd started coming in: the work-gangs selected for the first exploration work, most of them old hands of Rodney Maxwell's; the engineers they had recruited; Mohammed Matsui—he had a gang of his own, the same one he had been using in tearing down the converter at Tenth Army; the stockholders and officials; the press. And everybody else Tom Brangwyn's police hadn't been able to keep out.

The power plant was at the extreme bottom; Matsui began looking it over at once. Above it they found the service facilities—air-and-water plant; pumps for the artesian well;

sewage disposal. Then repair ships, and a laboratory, and laundries and kitchens above that.

"Where do you suppose it is?" Kurt Fawzi was asking. "Up at the very top, I suppose. Let's go up and work down; I can't wait till we've found it."

Like a kid on Christmas Eve, Conn thought. And there was no Santa Claus, and Christmas had been abolished.

The place was built in concentric circles, level above level. Combat equipment nearest the tunnel exit and nearest the vertical shaft, and ambulances and decontamination units and equipment for relief and rebuilding next. Storerooms, mile on circular mile of them. Not the hasty packrat cramming he'd seen at Tenth Army; everything had been brought in in order, carefully piled or racked, and then left. More stores for the next three levels up; then living quarters. Enlisted men's and women's quarters, no signs of occupancy. Enlisted kitchens and mess halls, untouched.

Most of the officers' quarters were similarly unused, but here and there some had been occupied. A sloppily made bed. A used cake of soap in the bathroom. An empty bottle in a closet. Officers' commissary stores had been used from and replaced; the officers' mess hall and kitchen had been in constant use, and the officers' club had a comfortably scuffed and lived-in look. There had been a few people there all the time of the War.

"Men and women, all officers or civilians," Klem Zareff said. "Didn't even have enlisted men to cook for them. And we haven't found a scrap of paper with writing on it, or an inch of recorded sound-tape or audiovisual film. Remember those big wire baskets, down at the mass-energy converters? Before they left, they disintegrated every scrap of writing or recording. This is where Merlin is; they were the people who worked with it."

And above, offices. General Staff. War Planning, with an incredibly complex star-map of the theater of war. Judge Advocate General. Inspector General. Service of Supply. They were full of computers, each one firing the hopes of people like Fawzi and Dolf Kellton and Judge Ledue, but they were only special-purpose machines, the sort to be found in any big business office. The Storisende Stock Exchange probably had much bigger ones.

Then they found big ones, rank on rank of cabinets, long consoles studded with lights and buttons, programming machines.

"It's Merlin!" Fawzi almost screamed. "We've found it!"

One of the reporters who had followed them in snatched his radio handphone from his belt and jabbered, then, realizing that the collapsium shielding kept him from getting out with it, he replaced it and bolted away.

"Hold it!" Conn yelled at the others, who were also becoming hysterical. "Wait till I take a look at this thing."

They managed to calm themselves. After all, he should know what it was; wasn't that why he'd gone to school on Terra? They followed him from machine to machine, first hopefully and then fearfully. Finally he turned, shaking his head and feeling like the doctor in a film show, telling the family that there's no hope for Grandpa.

"This is not Merlin. This is the personnel-file machine. It's taped for the records and data of every man and woman in the Third Force for the whole War. It's like the student-record machine at the University."

"Might have known it; this section in here's marked G-1 all over everything; that's personnel. Wouldn't have Merlin in here," Klem Zareff was saying.

"Well, we'll just keep on hunting for it till we do find it," Kurt Fawzi said. "It's here somewhere. It has to be."

The next level up was much smaller. Here were the offices of the top echelons of the Force Command Staff. They, unlike the ones below, had been used; from them, too, every scrap of writing or film or record-tape had vanished.

Finally, they entered the private office of Force-General Foxx Travis. It had not only been used, it was in disorder. Ashtrays full, many of the forty-year-old cigarette ends lipstick tinted. Chairs shoved around at random. Three bottles on the desk, with Terran bourbon labels; two empty and one with about an inch of whisky left in it. But no glasses.

That bothered Conn. Somehow, he couldn't quite picture the commander and staff of the Third Fleet-Army Force passing bottles around and drinking from the neck. Then he noticed that the wall across the room was strangely scarred and scratched. Dropping his eye to the floor under it, he caught the twinkle of broken glass. They had gathered here, and talked for a long time. Then they had risen, for a final toast, and when it was drunk, they had hurled their glasses against the wall and smashed them.

Then they had gone out, leaving the broken glass and the empty bottles; knowing that they would never return.

VIII

BEFORE THEY returned to the lower level into which the lateral tunnel entered, Matsui and his gang had the power plant going; the ventilator fans were humming softly, and whenever they pressed a starting button, the escalators began to move. They got the pumps going, and the oxygen-generators, and the sewage disposal system. Until the communication center could be checked and the relay station found, they ran a cable out to the *Lester Dawes*, landed in the canyon, and used her screen-and-radio equipment. Before the Claims Office in Storisende closed, Rodney Maxwell had transmitted in recorded views of the interior, and enough of a description for a final claim. They also received teleprint copies of the Storisende papers. The first story, in an extra edition of the *Herald-Guardian*, was headlined, MERLIN FOUND! That would have been the reporter who bolted off prematurely when they first saw the personnel record machines. Conn wondered if he still had a job. A later edition corrected this, but was full of extravagant accounts of what had been discovered. Merlin or no Merlin, Force Command Duplicate was the biggest abandoned-property discovery since the Third Force left the Trisystem.

63

The camp they had set up on top of the mesa was used, that night, only by Klem Zareff's guards. Everybody else was inside, eating cold rations when hungry and, when they could keep awake no longer, bedding down on piles of blankets or going up to the barracks rooms above.

The next day they found the relay station which rebroadcast signals from the buried aerial—or wouldn't one say, subterrial?—on top of the mesa. As Conn had expected, it was on top of a high butte three and a half miles to the south; it had been so skillfully camouflaged that none of the outlaw bands who roamed the Badlands had found it. After that, Force Command Duplicate was in communication with the rest of Poictesme.

They moved into the staff headquarters at the top; Foxx Travis's office, tidied up, became the headquarters for the company officials and chief supervisors. The workmen quartered themselves in the enlisted barracks, helping themselves liberally to anything they found. The crowds of sightseers kept swarming in, giving Tom Brangwyn's police plenty to do. Tom himself turned the marshal's office in Litchfield over to his chief deputy. Klem Zareff insisted on more men for his guard force. A dozen gunboats, eighty-foot craft mounting one 90-mm gun, several smaller auto-cannon and one missile-launcher, had been found; he took them over immediately, naming them for capital ships of the old System States Navy. It took some argument to dissuade him from repainting all of them black and green. He kept them all in the air, with a swarm of smaller airboats and combat-cars, circling the underground headquarters at a radius of a hundred miles. These patrols reported a general exodus from the region. At least a dozen outlaw bands, all with fast contragravity, had been camped inside the zone. Some fled at once; the rest needed only a few warning shots to send them away. Other bands, looking like legitimate prospecting parties, began to filter into the Badlands. Zareff came to Rodney Maxwell—instead of Kurt Fawzi, the titular head of the company, which was significant—to find out what policy regarding them would be.

"Well, we have no right to keep them out, as long as they stay outside our ten-mile radius," Conn's father said. "And

64

as we're the only thing that even looks like law around here, I'd say we have an obligation to give them protection. Have your boats investigate them; if they're legitimate, tell them they can call on us for help if they need it."

Conn protested, privately.

"There's a lot of stuff around here, in small caches," he said. "Equipment for guerrilla companies, in event of invasion. When work slacks off here, we could pick that stuff up."

"Conn, there's an old stock-market maxim: 'A bear can make money sometimes, and a bull can make money sometimes, but in the long run, a hog always loses.' Let the other people find some of this; it'll all help the Plan. Fact is, I've been thinking of leaking some information, if I can do it without Fawzi and that gang finding out. Do you know a good supply depot or something like that, say over on Acaire, or on the west coast? Big enough to be important, and to start a second prospectors' rush away from us."

"How about one of those hospitals?"

"No; not a hospital. We might use them to talk Wade Lucas into joining us. A lot of medical stores would be a good bait for him. I'm afraid he's going to make trouble if we don't do something about him."

"Well, how about engineering and construction equipment? I know where there's a lot of that, down to the southwest."

"That's farming country; that stuff'll be useful down there. I'll do that."

The next morning, Rodney Maxwell scorched the stratosphere to Storisende in his recon-car. The day after he got back, there was a big discovery of engineering equipment to the southwest and, as he had anticipated, a second rush of prospectors. They had the vertical shaft clear now, and the *Lester Dawes* was shuttling back and forth between Force Command Duplicate and Storisende. Other ships were coming in, now, mostly privately owned freighting ships. They bought almost anything, as fast as it came out.

The stock market had been paralyzed for a couple of days after the discovery of Force Command; nobody seemed to know what to sell and what to hold. Now it was going perfectly insane. Twenty or thirty new companies were being formed; unlike Litchfield Exploration & Salvage, they were all offering their stock to the public. A week after the opening of Force Command, the Stock Exchange reported the first half-million-share day since the War. A week after that, there were two million-share days in succession.

Some of the L. E. & S. stockholders who had come out on the first day began drifting back to Litchfield. Lester Dawes was the first to defect; there was nothing he could do at Force Command, and a great deal that needed his personal attention at the bank. Morgan Gatworth and Lorenzo Menardes and one or two others followed. Kurt Fawzi, however, refused to leave. Merlin was somewhere here at Force Command, he was sure of it, and he wasn't leaving till it was found. Neither were Franz Veltrin or Dolf Kellton or Judge Ledue. Tom Brangwyn resigned as town marshal; Klem Zareff was too busy even to think of Merlin; he had almost as many men under his command, and twice as much contragravity, as he had had when the System States Alliance Army had surrendered.

Conn flew to Litchfield, and found that the public works project had come to a stop at noon of the day when Force Command was entered, and that nothing had been done on it since. The cold vitrifier was still standing in the middle of the Mall, and topside Litchfield was littered in a dozen places with forsaken equipment and half-completed paving. There was no one in Kurt Fawzi's office in the Airlines Building, and the employment office was jammed with migratory workers vainly seeking jobs.

He hunted up Morgan Gatworth, the lawyer.

"Can't some of you get things started again?" he wanted to know. "This place is worse than it was before they started cleaning up."

"Yes, I know." Gatworth walked to an open window and looked down on the littered Mall. "But everybody just dropped everything as soon as you opened Force Command. Kurt Fawzi's not been back here since."

"Well, you're here. Lester Dawes and Lorenzo Menardes

are here. Why don't you just take over. Kurt Fawzi couldn't care less what you do; he's forgotten he is mayor of Litchfield. He's forgotten there is a Litchfield."

"Well, I don't like to just move into the mayor's office and take over. . . ."

From somewhere below, a submachine gun hammered. There were yells, pistol shots, and the submachine gun hammered again, a couple of short bursts.

"Some of the farm-tramps who can't get jobs, trying to steal something to eat, I suppose," Conn commented. Gatworth was frowning thoughtfully. He'd only need one more, very slight, push. "Why don't you talk to Wade Lucas. He's got brains, and he's honest—nobody but an honest man would have made himself as unpopular as Lucas has. If you pretend to be disillusioned with this Merlin business it might help convince him."

"He was blaming you and your father for what's been going on here in the last two weeks. Yes. He'd help get things straightened out."

At home, he found his mother simply dazed. She was happy to see him, and solicitous about his and his father's health. It seemed at times, though, as if he were somebody she had never met before. Events had gotten so far beyond her that she wasn't even trying to catch up.

Flora, returning from school, stopped short when she saw him.

"Well! I hope you like what you've done!" she greeted him.

"For a start, yes."

"For a start! You know what you've done?"

"Yes. I don't know what you think I've done, though. Tell me."

"You've turned everything into a madhouse; you've sent this whole world Merlin-crazy. Look at the stock market. . . ."

"You look at it. All I can see is a pack of lunatics playing Russian roulette with five chambers loaded out of six. Some of this so-called stock that's being peddled around isn't worth five millisols a share—Seekers for Merlin, Ltd., closed today at a hundred and seventy. You notice, there isn't any L. E.

67

& S. being traded. If you don't believe me, talk to Lester Dawes; he'll tell you what we think of this market."

"Well, it's your fault!"

"In part it's my fault that any of these quarter-wits have any money to play the market with. They wouldn't have money enough to play a five-centisol slot machine if we hadn't gotten a little business started."

There was just a little truth to that, too. A few woolen socks were coming out from under mattresses, and a few tin cans were being exhumed in cellars, since the new flood of Federation equipment and supplies had gotten on the market. He'd seen a freshly lettered sign on Len Yeniguchi's tailor shop: QUARTER PRICE IN FEDERATION CURRENCY.

That night, however, he had one of the nightmares he used to have as a child—a dream of climbing up onto a huge machine and getting it started, and then clinging, helpless and terrified, unable to stop it as it went faster and faster toward destruction.

Klem Zareff's patrols were encountering larger outlaw bands, the result of gang mergers. They were fighting with prospecting parties, and prospecting parties were fighting one another. Much of this was making the newscasts. One battle, between two regularly chartered prospecting companies, lasted three days, with an impressive casualty list.

Public demands were growing that the Planetary Government do something about the situation; the Government was wondering what to do, or how. There were indignant questions in Parliament. Finally, the Government dragged a couple of armed ships off Mothball Row—a combat freighter like the *Lester Dawes,* and a big assault transport—and began trying to get them into commission.

And, of course, the market boom was still on. The newscasts were full of that, too. He had started worrying about *if* a bust came; now he was worrying about what would happen *when* it did. Another good reason for wanting to get to Koshchei and getting a hypership built; when the bust came, he and his father would want one, very badly.

In any case, it was time to begin getting an expedition

ready for Barathrum Spaceport. Quite a few of the new companies had large contragravity craft, and the nascent Planetary Air Navy was approaching a state of being. He wanted to get out there before anybody else did.

Maybe if they got the hypership built soon enough, it would start a second, sound boom that would cushion the crash of the present speculative market when it came, as come it must.

He talked to Klem Zareff about borrowing a couple of the eighty-foot gunboats. Zareff's attitude was automatically negative.

"We mustn't weaken our defense-perimeter; we'd be inviting disaster. Why, this whole country in here is simply swarming with outlaws. They fired on one of our gunboats, the *Werewolf*, yesterday."

He'd heard about that; somebody had launched a missile from the ground, and the *Werewolf* had detonated it with a counter-missile. It had probably been some legitimate prospecting company who'd taken the L. E. & S. craft for a pirate.

"And there was a battle down in the Devil's Pigpen day before yesterday."

That had been outlaws; they had been annihilated by something calling itself Seekers for Merlin, Ltd., whose stock was still skyrocketing on the Exchange. He mentioned that.

"These other prospecting companies are doing a lot of our outlaw-fighting for us, and as long as the country's full of small independent parties, the outlaws go after them and leave us alone."

"Yes, and I have my doubts about a lot of these prospecting companies, and a lot of the outlaws, too," Zareff said. "I think a lot of both are Federation agents; they're waiting till we find Merlin, and then they'll all jump us."

"Well," Conn adjusted his argument to the old Rebel's obsession, "I'll admit that, as a possibility. If so, we'll need heavier weapons than we have. This spaceport on Barathrum might be just the place to get them."

"Yes. It might. Defense armament, and stored ships' weapons. Say, if we grab that place and move all the heavy guns and missiles here, we could stand off anybody." The thought

69

of a fight with minions of the Terran Federation seemed to have shaved ten years off his age in a twinkling. "You take the *Lester Dawes*, and, let's say, three of these gunboats. Let me see. *Goblin*, Fred Karski. And *Vampire*, Charley Gatworth. And *Dragon*, Stefan Jorisson. They're all good men. Home Guard; trained them myself."

"Aren't you coming, Colonel?"

"Oh, I'd like to, Conn, but I can't. I don't want to be away from here; no telling what might happen. But you keep in constant screen-contact; if you get into any trouble, I'll come with everything I can put into the air."

IX

BARATHRUM was a grim land, naked black and gray. Spines and crags of bare rock jutted up, lava-flows like black glaciers twisting among them. It was split by faults and fissures, pimpled with ash-cones. Except for the seabirds that nested among the cliffs and the few thin patches of green where seeds windblown from the mainland had taken root, it was as lifeless as when some ancient convulsion had thrust it up from the sea. Barathrum was a dead Inferno, untenanted even by the damned; by comparison, the Badlands seemed lushly fertile.

The four craft crossed above the line of white breakers that marked the division of sea and land; the gunboat *Goblin* in the lead, her sisters, *Vampire* and *Dragon* to right and left and a little behind, and the *Lester Dawes* a few miles in the rear. Fred Karski was at the *Goblin*'s controls; Conn, beside him, was peering ahead into the teleview screen and shifting his eyes from it to the map and back again.

Somebody behind him was saying that it would be a nice place to be air-wrecked. Somebody else was telling him not to joke about it. From the radio, his father was asking: "Can you see it, yet?"

"Not yet. We're on the right map-and-compass direction; we should before long."

"We're picking up radiation," Fred Karski said. "Way above normal count. I hope the place isn't hot."

"We're getting that, too," Rodney Maxwell said. "Looks like power radiation; something must be on there."

After forty years, that didn't seem likely. He leaned over to look at the omnigeiger, then whistled. If that was normal leakage from inactive power units, there must be enough of them to power ten towns the size of Litchfield.

"Something's operating there," he said, and then realized what that meant. Somebody had beaten them to the spaceport. That would be one of the new companies formed after the opening of Force Command. He was wishing, now, that he hadn't let himself be talked out of coming here first. Older and wiser heads indeed!

Fred Karski whistled shrilly into his radio phone. "Attention everybody! General alert. Prepare for combat; prepare to take immediate evasive action. We must assume that the spaceport is occupied, and that the occupants are hostile. Captain Poole, will you please make ready aboard your ship? Reduce both speed and altitude, and ready your guns and missiles at once."

"Well, now, wait a minute, young fellow," Poole began to argue. "You don't know—"

"No. I don't. And I want all of us alive after we find out, too," Karski replied.

Rodney Maxwell's voice, in the background, said something indistinguishable. Poole said ungraciously, "Well, all right, if you think so . . ."

The *Lester Dawes* began dropping to the rear and going down toward the ground. Conn returned to the teleview screen in time to see the truncated cone of the extinct volcano rise on the horizon, dwarfing everything around it. Fred Karski was talking to Colonel Zareff, back at Force Command, giving him the radiation count.

"That's occupied," the old soldier replied. "Mass-energy

71

converter going. Now, Fred, don't start any shooting unless you have to, but don't get yourself blown to MC waiting on them to fire the first shot."

The dark cone bulked higher and higher in the screen. It must be seven miles around the crater, and a mile deep; when that thing blew out, ten or fifteen thousand years ago, it must have been something to see, preferably from a ship a thousand miles off-planet. It was so huge that it was hard to realize that the jumbled foothills around it were themselves respectably lofty mountains.

When they were within five miles of it, something twinkled slightly near the summit. An instant later, the missileman, in his turret overhead, shouted:

"Missile coming up; counter-missile off!"

"Grab onto something, everybody!" Karski yelled, bracing himself in his seat.

Conn, on his feet, flung his arms around an upright stanchion and hung on. Fred's hand gave a twisting jerk on the steering handle; the *Goblin* went corkscrewing upward. In the rearview screen, Conn saw a pink fireball blossom far below. The sound and the shock-wave never reached them; the *Goblin* outran them. *Dragon* and *Vampire* were spiraling away in opposite directions. The radio was loud with voices, and a few of the words were almost printable. A gong began clanging from the command post on top of the mesa on the mainland.

"Be quiet, all of you!" Klem Zareff was bellowing. "And get back from there. Back three or four miles; close enough so they won't dare use thermonuclears. Take cover behind one of those ridges, where they can't detect you. Then we can start figuring what the Gehenna to do next."

That made sense. And get it settled who's in command of this Donnybrook, while we're at it, Conn thought. He looked into the rear-and sideview screens, and taking cover immediately made even more sense. Two more fireballs blossomed, one dangerously close to the *Dragon*. Guns were firing from the mountaintop, too, big ones, and shells were bursting close to them. He saw a shell land on and another beside one of the enemy gun positions—115-mm's from the

Lester Dawes, he supposed. He continued to cling to the stanchion, and the *Goblin* shot straight up, and he was expecting to see the sky blacken and the stars come out when the gunboat leveled and started circling down again. The mountainside, he saw, was sending up a lightning-crackling tower of smoke and dust that swelled into a mushroom top.

Klem Zareff, on the radio, was demanding to know who'd launched that.

"We did, sir; *Dragon*," Stefan Jorisson was replying. "We had to get rid of it. We took a hit. Gun turret's smashed, Milt Hennant's dead, and Abe Samuels probably will be before I'm done talking, and if we get this crate down in one piece, it'll do for a miracle till a real one happens."

"Well, be careful how you shoot those things off," his father implored, from the *Lester Dawes*. "Get one inside the crater and we won't have any spaceport."

The *Lester Dawes* vanished behind a mountain range a few miles from the volcano. The *Dragon*, still airborne but in obvious difficulties, was limping after her, and the *Vampire* was covering the withdrawal, firing rapidly but with doubtful effect with her single 90-mm and tossing out counter-missiles. There was another fireball between her and the mountain. Then, when the *Dragon* had followed the *Lester Dawes* to safety, she turned tail and bolted, the *Goblin* following. As they approached the mountains, something the shape of a recon-car and about half the size passed them going in the opposite direction. As they dropped into chasm on the other side, another nuclear went off at the volcano.

When Conn and Fred left the *Goblin* and boarded the ship, they found Rodney Maxwell, Captain Poole, and a couple of others on the bridge. Charley Gatworth, the skipper of the *Vampire*, Morgan Gatworth's son, was with them, and, imaged in a screen, so was Klem Zareff. One of the other screens, from a pickup on the *Vampire*, showed the *Dragon* lying on her side, her turret crushed and her gun, with the muzzle-brake gone, bent upward. A couple of lorries from the *Lester Dawes* were alongside; as Conn watched, a blanket-wrapped body, and then another, were lowered from the disabled gunboat.

73

"Fred, how are you and Charley fixed for counter-missiles?" Zareff was asking. "Get loaded up with them off the ship, as many as you can carry. Charley, you go up on top of this ridge above, and take cover where you can watch the mountain. Transmit what you see back to the ship. Fred, you take a position about a quarter way around from where you are now. Don't let them send anything over, but don't start anything yourselves. I'm coming out with everything I can gather up here; I'll be along myself in a couple of hours, and the rest will be stringing in after me. In the meantime, Rodney, you're in command."

Well, that settled that. There was one other point, though.

"Colonel," Conn said, "I assume that this spaceport is occupied by one of these new prospecting companies. We have no right to take it away from them, have we?"

"They fired on us without warning," Karski said. "They killed Milt, and it's ten to one Abe won't live either. We owe them something for that."

"We do, and we'll pay off. Conn, you assume wrong. This gang's been at the spaceport long enough to get the detection system working and put the defense batteries on ready. They didn't do that since this morning, and up to last evening they neglected to file claim. I'll assume they're on the wrong side of the law. They're outlaws, Conn. All the raids along the east coast; everybody's blamed them on the Badlands gangs. I'll admit they're responsible for some of it, but I'll bet this gang at the spaceport is doing most of it."

That was reasonable. Barathrum was closer to the scene of the worst outlaw depredations than the Badlands, not more than an hour at Mach Two. And nobody ever though of Barathrum as an outlaw hangout. People rarely thought of Barathrum at all. He liked the idea. The only thing against it was that he wanted so badly to believe it.

They brought the body of Milt Hennant aboard, and Abe Samuels, swathed in bandages and immobilized by narcotic injections. A few more of the *Dragon's* six-man crew had been injured. Jorrisson, the skipper, had one trouser leg slit to the belt and his right thigh splinted and bandaged; he took over the *Lester Dawes'* missile controls, which he could manage sitting in one place. Fred Karski and Charley Gatworth went aboard their craft and lifted out.

For a long time, nothing happened. Conn got out the plans of the volcano spaceport and the photomaps of the surrounding area. The principal entrance, the front door of the spaceport, was the crater of the extinct volcano itself. It was ringed, outside, with launching-sites and gun positions, and according to the data he had, some of the guns were as big as 250-mm. How many outlaws there were to man them was a question a lot of people could get killed trying to answer. The ship docks and shops were down on the level of the crater floor, in caverns, both natural and excavated, that extended far back into the mountain. There were two galleries, one above the other, extending entirely around the inside of the crater near the top; passages from them gave access to the outside gun and missile positions.

With a dozen ships the size of the *Lester Dawes*, about five thousand men, and a CO who wasn't concerned with trivialities like casualties, they could have taken the place in half an hour. With what they had, trying to fight their way in at the top was out of the question.

There was another way in. He had known about it from the beginning, and he was trying desperately to think of a way not to utilize it. It was a tunnel two miles long, running into some of the bottom workshops and storerooms back of the ship berths from a big blowhole or small crater at the foot of the mountain. According to the fifty-year-old plans, it was big enough to take a gunboat in, and on paper it looked like a royal highway straight to the heart of the enemy's stronghold.

To Conn, it looked like a wonderful place to commit suicide. He'd only had a short introductory course, in one semester, in military and protective robotics, just enough to give him a foundation if he wanted to go into that branch of the subject later. It was also enough to give him an idea of the sort of booby-traps that tunnel could be filled with. He knew what he'd have put into it if he'd been defending that place.

Colonel Zareff had sent one last message from Force

Command when he lifted off with a flight of recon-cars. After that, he maintained a communication blackout. It was an hour and a half before he got close enough to be detected from the outlaw stronghold. Immediately, the volcano began spewing out missiles. Poole hastily took the *Lester Dawes* ten miles down the rift-valley in sixty seconds, while Stefan Jorisson put out a nuclear-warhead missile and left it circling about where the ship had been. From their respective positions, Fred Karski and Charley Gatworth filled the airspace midway to the volcano with counter-missiles, each loaded with four rockets. There were explosions, fireballs in the air and rising cumulus clouds of varicolored smoke and dust. Only about half the enemy missiles reached the *Lester Dawes'* former position.

When their controllers, back at the volcano, couldn't see the ship in their screens, the missiles bunched together. Immediately, Jorisson sent his missile up to join them and detonated it. Including his own, eight nuclear weapons went off together in a single blast that shook the ground like an earthquake and churned the air like a hurricane. Klem Zareff came on-screen at once.

"Now what did you do?" he demanded. "Blew the whole place up, didn't you?"

Rodney Maxwell told him. Zareff laughed. "They might just think they got the ship; all the pickups would be smashed before they could see what really happened. You're about ten miles south of that? Be with you in a few minutes."

They got a screen on for his rearview pickup. Zareff had with him a dozen recon-cars, some of them under robo-control; six gunboats followed, and behind them, to the horizon, other craft were strung out—airboats, troop carriers, and freight-scows. They could see enemy missiles approaching in Zareff's front screen; counter-missiles got most of them, and a couple of pilotless recon-cars were sacrificed. The *Lester Dawes* blasted more missiles as they crossed the top of the mountain range. Then Zareff's car was circling in and entering at one of the ship's open cargo-ports. Zareff and Anse Dawes got out.

"Gunboats are only half an hour behind," Zareff said.

"Get some screens on to them, Anse; you know the combinations. Now let's see what kind of a mess we're in here."

It was almost a miracle, the way the tottering old man Conn had seen on the dock at Litchfield when he had arrived from Terra had been rejuvenated.

The rest of the reinforcements arrived slowly, sending missiles and counter-missiles out ahead of them. Zareff began worrying about the supply; the enemy didn't seem to be running short. By 1300—Conn noted the time incredulously; the battle seemed to have been going on forever, instead of just four hours—the *Lester Dawes* had moved halfway around the volcano and was almost due west of it, and the eight gunboats were spaced all around the perimeter. Then one stopped transmitting; in the other screens, there was a rising fireball where she had been. The radio was loud with verbal reports.

"*Poltergeist,*" Zareff said, naming half a dozen names. One or two of them had been schoolmates of Conn's at the Academy; he knew how he'd feel about it later, but now it simply didn't register.

"They're launching missiles faster than we can shoot them down," he said.

"That's usually the beginning of the end," Zareff said. "I saw it happen too often during the War. We've got to get inside that place. It's a lot of harmless fun to send contragravity robots out to smash each other, but it doesn't win battles. Battles are won by men, standing with their feet on the ground, using personal weapons."

"We'll have to win this one pretty soon," Rodney Maxwell said. "The amount of nuclear energy we've been releasing will be detectable anywhere on the planet by now. The Government has a ship like the *Lester Dawes* in commission; if this keeps on, she'll be coming out for a look."

"Then we'll have help," Captain Poole said.

"We need Government help like we need the polka-dot fever," Rodney Maxwell said. "If they get in it, they'll claim the spaceport themselves, and we'll have fought a battle for nothing."

Well, that was it, then. The spaceport was essential to the

Maxwell Plan. He'd gotten seven men killed—eight, if the recon-car that was taking Abe Samuels to the hospital in Litchfield didn't make it in time—and it was up to him to see that they hadn't died for nothing. He spread the photo-map and the spaceport plans on the chart table.

"Look at this," he said.

Klem Zareff looked at it. He didn't like it any better than Conn had. He studied the plan for a moment, chewing his cigar.

"You know, it's possible they don't know that thing exists," he said, without too much conviction. "You'll be betting the lives of at least twenty men; fewer than that couldn't accomplish anything."

"I'll be putting mine on the table along with them," Conn said. "I'll lead them in."

He was wishing he hadn't had to say that. He did, though. It was the only thing he could say.

"You better pick the men to go with me, Colonel," he continued. "You know them better than I do. We'll need working equipment, too; I have no idea what we may have to take out of the way, inside."

"I won't call for volunteers," Zareff said. "I'll pick Home Guards; they did their volunteering when they joined."

"Let me pick one man, Colonel," Anse Dawes said. "I'll pick me."

X

THEY SENT a snooper in first; it picked up faint radiation leakage from inactive power units of overhead lights, and nothing else. The tunnel stretched ahead of it, empty, and dark beyond its infrared vision. After it had gone a mile without triggering anything, the jeep followed Anse Dawes piloting and Conn at the snooper controls watching what it transmitted back. The two lorries followed, loaded with men and equipment, and another jeep brought up the rear. They had cut screen-and-radio communication with the outside; they weren't even using inter-vehicle communication.

At length, the snooper emerged into a big cavern, swinging slowly to scan it. The walls and ceiling were rough and irregular; it was natural instead of excavated. Only the floor had been leveled smooth. There were a lot of things in it, machinery and vehicles, all battered and in poor condition, dusty and cobwebbed: the spaceport junkheap. A passage, still large enough for one of the gunboats, led deeper into the mountain toward the crater. They sent the snooper in and, after a while, followed.

They came to other rectangular, excavated caverns. On the plans, they were marked as storerooms. Cases and crates, indeterminate shrouded objects; some had never been disturbed, but here and there they found evidence of recent investigation.

Beyond was another passage, almost as wide as the Mall in Litchfield; even the *Lester Dawes* could have negotiated it. According to the plans, it ran straight out to the ship docks and the open crater beyond. Anse turned the jeep into a side passage, and Conn recalled the snooper and sent it ahead. On the plan, it led to another natural cavern, half its width shown as level with the entrance. The other half was a pit, marked as sixty feet deep; above this and just under the ceiling, several passages branched out in different directions.

The snooper reported visible light ahead; fluoroelectric light from one of the upper passages, and firelight from the pit. The air-analyzer reported woodsmoke and a faint odor of burning oil. He sent the snooper ahead, tilting it to look down into the pit.

A small fire was burning in the center; around it, in a circle, some hundred and fifty people, including a few women and children, sat, squatted or reclined. A low hum of voices came out of the soundbox.

"Who the blazes are they?" Anse whispered. "I can't see any way they could have gotten down there."

They were in rags, and they weren't armed; there wasn't so much as a knife or a pistol among them. Conn motioned the lorries and the other jeep forward.

"Prisoners," he said. "I think they were hauled down here on a scow, shoved off, and left when the fighting started. Cover me," he told the men in the lorries. "I'm going down and talk to them."

Somebody below must have heard something. As Anse took the jeep over and started floating it down, the circle around the fire began moving, the women and children being pushed to the rear and the men gathering up clubs and other chance weapons. By the time the jeep grounded, the men in the pit were standing defensively in front of the women and children.

They were all dirty and ragged; the men were unshaven. There was a tall man with a grizzled beard, in greasy coveralls; another man with a black beard and an old Space Navy uniform, his head bandaged with a dirty and blood-caked rag; another in the same uniform, wearing a cap on which the Terran Federation insignia had been replaced by the emblem of Transcontinent & Overseas Shiplines and the words CHIEF ENGINEER. And beside the tall man with the gray beard, was a girl in baggy trousers and a torn smock. Like the others, she was dirty, but in spite of the rags and filth, Conn saw that she was beautiful. Black hair, dark eyes, an impudently tilted nose.

They all looked at him in hostility that gradually changed to perplexity and then hope.

"Who are you?" the tall man with the gray beard asked. "You're none of this gang here."

"Litchfield Exploration & Salvage; I'm Conn Maxwell."

That meant nothing; none of them had been near a newsscreen lately.

"What's going on topside?" the man with the bandaged head and the four stripes on his sleeve asked. "There was firing, artillery and nuclears, and they herded us down here. Have you cleaned the bloody murderers out?"

"We're working on it," Conn said. "I take it they aren't friends of yours?"

Foolish Question of the Year; they all made that evident.

"They took my ship; they murdered my first officer and half my crew and passengers . . ."

They burned our home and killed our servants," the girl said. "They kidnapped my father and me . . ."

"They've been keeping us here as slaves."

"It's the Blackie Perales gang," the tall man with the gray beard said. "They've been making us work for them, converting a blasted tub of a contragravity ship into a spacecraft. I beg your pardon, Captain Nichols; she was a fine ship—for her intended purpose."

"You're Captain Nichols?" Anse Dawes exclaimed. "Of the *Harriet Barne?*"

"That's right. The *Harriet Barne's* here; they've been making us work on her, to convert her to an interplanetary craft, of all idiotic things."

"My name's Yves Jacquemont," the man with the gray beard said. "I'm a retired hyperspace maintenance engineer; I had a little business at Waterville, buying, selling and rebuilding agricultural machinery. This gang found out about me; they raided and burned our village and carried me and my daughter, Sylvie, away. We've been working for them for the last four months, tearing Captain Nichols' ship down and armoring her with collapsium."

"How many pirates are there here?"

That started an argument. Nobody was quite sure; two hundred and fifty seemed to be the highest estimate, which Conn decided to play safe by accepting.

"You get us out of here," Yves Jacquemont was saying. "All we want is a chance at them."

"How about arms? You can't do much with clubs and fists."

"Don't worry about that; we know where to get arms. The treasure house, where they store their loot. There's plenty of arms and ammunition, and anything else you can think of. They've used us to help stow the stuff; we know where it is."

"Anse, you remember those scows we saw, in the big room before we came to the broad passage? Take four men in the jeep; have them lift two of them and bring them here. Then, you get out to the end of the tunnel and call the *Lester Dawes*. Tell them what's happened, tell them they can get gunboats all the way in, and wait to guide them when they arrive."

When Anse turned and climbed into the jeep, he asked Yves Jacquemont: "Why does this Perales want an interplanetary ship?"

"He's crazy!" Jacquemont swore. "Paranoid; megalomaniac. He talks of organizing all the pirates and outlaws on the planet into one band and making himself king. He's heard that there are Space Navy superweapons on Koshchei—I suppose there are, at that—and he wants to get a lot of planetbusters and hellburners and annihilators." He lowered his voice. "Captain Nichols and I were going to fix up something that'd blow the *Harriet Barne* up as soon as he got her out of atmosphere."

He talked for a while to Jacquemont and his daughter Sylvie, and to Nichols and the chief engineer, whose name was Vibart. There was evidently nothing else at the spaceport of which a spaceship could be built, but there were foundries and rolling-mills and a collapsed-matter producer. The *Harriet Barne* was gutted, half torn down, and half armored with new collapsium-plated sheet steel. It might be possible to continue the work on her and take her to space.

Then the two scows floated over the top of the pit and began letting down. They got the prisoners into them, the combat-effective men in one and the women and children in the other. At the top, he took over the remaining jeep, getting Jacquemont, his daughter, and the two contragravityship officers in with him.

"Up to the top," Jacquemont said. "Take the middle passage, and turn right at the next intersection."

As they approached the section where the pirates stored their loot, the sound of guns and explosions grew louder, and they began picking up radio and screen signals, all of which were scrambled and incomprehensible. The pirates, in different positions, talking among themselves. With all that, it ought to be safe to use their own communication equipment; nobody would notice it.

The treasuure room looked like a giant pack rat's nest. Cases and crates of merchandise, bales, boxes, barrels. Machinery. Household and industrial robots. The prisoners piled out of the two scows and began rummaging. Somebody found a case of cigarettes and smashed it open; in a moment, cartons were being tossed around and opened, and everybody was smoking. The pirates evidently hadn't issued any tobacco rations to their prisoners.

And they found arms and ammunition, began ripping open cases, handing out rifles, pistols, submachine guns. The prisoners grabbed them even more hungrily than the cigarettes. Sylvie Jacquemont took charge of the ammunition; she had three men opening boxes for her, while she passed out boxes of cartridges and made sure that everybody had ammunition to fit their weapons. A ragged man who might have been a farm-tramp or a rich planter before his capture had gotten a bale of cloth open and was tossing rags around while the chief engineer inspected weapons and showed people how to clean out the cosmoline and fill their spare magazines.

Conn collected a few of his own party.

"Let's look these robots over," he said. "Find about half a dozen we can load with blasting explosive and send ahead of us on contragravity."

They found several—an electric-light servicer, a couple of wall-and-window washers, a serving-robot that looked as if it had come from a restaurant, and an all-purpose robojanitor. In the passage outside, they began loading the lorries with bricks of ionite and packages of cataclysmite, packing all the scrap-iron and other junk around the explosives that they could. As soon as they had weapons, the prisoners came swarming out, making more noise than was necessary and a good deal more than was safe. Sylvie Jacquemont, with a submachine gun slung from one shoulder and a canvas bag of spare magazines from the other, came over to see what he was doing.

"Well, look what you're doing to him!" she mock-reproached-ed. "That's a dirty trick to play on a little robot!"

He grinned at her. "You and my mother would get along. She always treats robots like people."

"Well, they are, sort of. They aren't alive—at least, I don't think they are—but they do what you tell them, and they learn tricks, and they have personalities."

That was true. He didn't think robots were alive, either, though biophysics professors tended to become glibly evasive when pinned down to defining life. Robots could learn, if you used the term loosely enough. And any robot with more than five hundred hours service picked up a definite and often exasperating personality.

"I've been working with them, and tearing them down and fixing them, ever since I was in pigtails," she added.

The half-dozen natural leaders among the prisoners—Jacquemont and his daughter, the two *Harriet Barne* officers, and a couple of others—bent over the photoprinted plans Conn had, located their position, and told him as much as they could about what lay ahead. Sylvie Jacquemont could handle robots; she would ride in the front seat of the jeep while he piloted. Vibart, the chief engineer, and Yves Jacquemont would ride behind. Nichols would ride in the scow with the fighting men. One lorry of his own party would follow the jeep; the other would bring up the rear.

He snapped on the screen and punched the ship combination. Stefan Jorisson appeared in it.

"Hi, Conn! You all right?" He raised his voice. "Conn's onscreen!"

His father appeared at Jorisson's shoulder and, a moment later, Klem Zareff.

"Well, we're in, all right," he said. "We just picked up an army, too." He swung the jeep to get the crowd in the pickup, explaining who they were. "Did you hear from Anse?"

"Yes, he just screened in," Rodney Maxwell said. "He said a gunboat can get in."

"That's right; clear into the crater."

"Well, we're going to put three of them inside," Zareff told him. "*Werewolf, Zombi,* and *Dero*. And a troop carrier with fifty men; flamethrowers, portable machine guns, bomb-launchers; regular special-weapons section. What can you do where you are?"

"Here? Nothing. We're going to work around to the other

side of the crater, and then find a vertical shaft and go up topside and make as much disturbance as we can."

"That's it!" Zareff approved. "Pull them off balance; as soon as we get in, we'll go straight to the top. Look for us in about an hour; it's going to take time getting to the tunnel-mouth without being spotted from above."

He lifted the jeep and started off; the lorry, and the scows and the other lorry followed; the snooper and the bomb-robots went ahead like a pack of hunting dogs. They went through great chambers, dark and silent and bulking with dusty machines. Jacquemont explained that the prisoners had never gotten into this section; the *Harriet Barne* was a mile or so to their right. Conn turned left, when the noise of firing from outside became plainer. A foundry. A machine-shop which seemed to have been abandoned in the middle of some rush job that hadn't really been necessary. They came to a place even the snooper couldn't enter, choked to the ceiling with dead vegetation, hydroponic seed-plants that had been left untended to grow wild and die. They emerged into outside light, in vast caves a mile high and open onto the crater, and looked across the floor that had been leveled and vitrified to the other side, three and a half miles away.

He didn't know whether to be more awed by the original eruption that had formed the crater or by the engineering feat of carving these docks and ship-berths, big enough for the hugest hyperspaceship, into it.

At first, he had been afraid of getting into position too soon before the task force from outside could profit by the diversion. Then he began to worry about the time it was taking to get halfway around the crater. He could hear artillery thundering continuously above. Except at the very beginning of the battle, there had been little gunfire. He wondered if both sides were running out of lift-and-drive missiles, or if the fighting had gotten too close for anybody to risk using nuclear weapons.

He was also worrying about the women and children among the released prisoners.

"Why did the pirates bother with them?" he asked Sylvie.

"They used the women and some of the old men to do

housekeeping chores for them," she said. "Mostly, though, they were hostages; if the men didn't work, Perales threatened to punish the women and children. I wasn't doing any housework; I'm too good a mechanic. I was helping on the ship."

"Well, what'll I do with them when the fighting starts? I can't take them into battle."

"You'll have to; it'll be the safest place for them. You can't leave them anywhere and risk having them recaptured."

"That means we'll have to detach some men to cover them, and that'll cut our striking force down." He whistled at the sound-pickup of his screen and told his father about it. "What do I do with these people, anyhow?"

"You're the officer in command, Conn," his father told him. "Your decision. How soon can you attack? We're almost through to the crater."

"There's a vertical shaft right above us, and a lot of noise at the top. We'll send up a couple of bomb-robots to clear things at the shaft-head and follow with everything we have."

"Noncombatants and all?"

He nodded. "Only thing we can do." An old quotation occurred to him. " 'If you want to make an omelet, you have to break eggs.' "

He wondered who'd said that in the first place. One of the old Pre-Atomic conquerors; maybe Hitler. No, Hitler would have said, "If you want to make sauerkraut, you have to chop cabbage." Maybe it was Caesar.

"We'd better send Gumshoe Gus up, first," Sylvie suggested.

"You handle him. Take a quick look around, and then pull him back. We'll need him later." It was the first time he'd ever caught himself calling a robot "him," instead of "it." He thought for a second, and added: "Give your father and Mr. Vibart the controls for the two window-washers; you handle the snooper."

He gave more instructions: Yves Jacquemont to turn his bomb-robot right, Vibart to turn his left; the two lorries to follow the jeep up the shaft, the scows to follow. Then he leaned back and looked at the screens that had been rigged under the top of the jeep. A circle of light appeared in one, growing larger and brighter as the snooper approached the top of the shaft; two more came on as the bomb-robots followed.

"All right; follow me," he said into the inter-vehicle radio, and started the jeep slowly up the shaft.

The snooper popped out of the shaft, onto a gallery that had been cut into the solid rock, fifty feet high and a hundred and fifty across, with a low parapet on the outside and the mile-deep crater beyond. There were a few grounded air-cars and lorries in sight, and a medium airboat rested a hundred or so feet to the right of the shaft-opening. Fifteen or twenty men were clustered around it, with a lifter loaded with ammunition. They looked like any crowd of farm-tramps. Suddenly, one of them saw the snooper, gave a yell, and fired at it with a rifle. Sylvie pulled it back into the shaft; her father and the chief engineer sent the two bomb-robots up onto the gallery. The right-hand robot sped at the airboat; the last thing Conn saw in its screen was a face, bearded and villainous and contorted with fright, looking out the pilot's window of the airboat. Then it went dead, and there was a roar from above. On the other side, several men were firing straight at the pickup of the other robot; it went dead, too, and there was a second explosion.

In the communication screen, somebody was yelling, "Give them another one for Milt Hennant!" and his father was urging him to get in fast, before they recovered.

In peace or war, screen communication was a wonderful thing. The only trouble was that it let in too many kibitzers.

The gallery, when the jeep emerged onto it, was empty except for casualties, a few still alive. The side of the airboat was caved in; the lifter-load of ammunition had gone up with the bomb. He moved the jeep to the right of the shaft and waited for the vehicles behind him, suffering a brief indecision.

Never divide your force in the presence of the enemy.

There had been generals who had done that and gotten away with it, but they'd had names like Foxx Travis and Robert E. Lee and Napoleon—Napoleon; that was who'd made that crack about omelets! They'd known what they were doing. He was playing this battle by ear.

There was a lot of shouting ahead to the right. That meant live pirates, a deplorable situation which ought to be corrected at once. The communication screen was noisy, now; his father had gotten to the top gallery with the three gun cutters, and was meeting resistance. He formed his column, his jeep and one of the lorries in front, the scows next, and the second lorry behind, and started around the gallery counterclockwise, the snoopers and the three remaining bomb-robots ahead. They began running into resistance almost at once.

Bullets spatted on the armor glass in front of him, spalling it and blotching it with metal until he found that he could steer better by the show-back of his view-pickup. He used that until the pickup was shot out. Then his father began wanting to know, from the communication screen, what was going on and where he was. A bomb or something went off directly under the jeep, bouncing it almost to the ceiling; he found that it was impossible to lift it again after it settled to the floor of the gallery, and they all piled out to fight on foot. Sommers and his gang from the number one lorry were also afoot; their vehicle had been disabled. He saw them lifting wounded into one of the scows.

They blew up the light-service robot to clear a nest of pirates who had taken cover ahead of them. They sent the robo-janitor up a side passage and exploded it in a missile-launching position on the outside of the mountain; that produced a tremendous explosion. They began running out of cartridges, and had to stop and glean more from enemy casualties. They expended their last bomb-robot, the restaurant server, to break up another pirate resistance point.

At length he found himself, with Sylvie and her father and one of the Home Guardsmen from Sommers' lorry, lying behind an aircar somebody had knocked out with a bazooka, with two dead pirates for company and a dozen distressingly live ones ahead behind an improvised barricade. Behind, there was frantic firing; the rear-guard seemed to have run into trouble, probably from some gang that had come down from the upper level. He wondered what his father was doing with the gunboats; since abandoning the jeep, he had lost his only means of contact.

Suddenly, the men in front jumped up from their barricade and came running toward him. Been reinforced, now they're counterattacking. His rifle was empty; he drew his pistol and shot one of them, and then he saw that they were throwing up their hands and yelling for quarter. This was something new.

He looked around quickly, to make sure none of the liberated prisoners except Jacquemont and his daughter were around, and then called to a couple of his own men to come up and help him. While they were relieving the pirates of their pistol belts and cartridge bandoliers, more came up, their hands over their heads, herded by a combat car from which Tom Brangwyn covered them with a pair of 12-mm machine guns. Tom hadn't put in an appearance before he had taken his commando force into the tunnel; he hadn't even known the chief of Company Police was on Barathrum.

"Well, nice seeing you," he greeted. "How did you get in?"

"Over the top," Brangwyn told him. "Everything's caved in on the other side. We have a quarter of the top gallery, and half of this one. Your father's cleaning up above. Klem's got some men working along the outside."

Sylvie was tugging at his arm. "Hey, look! Look at that!" she was clamoring. "Who's she belong to?"

He looked; the *Lester Dawes* was coming over the edge of the crater.

"She's ours," he said. "It's all over but the mopping up. And counting the egg breakage."

XI

THE SHOOTING died down to occasional rattles of small arms, usually followed by yells for quarter. An explosion thundered from across the crater. The *Lester Dawes* fired her big guns a few times. A machine gun stuttered. A pistol banged, far away. It took two hours before all the pirates had been hunted out of hiding and captured, or killed if found by their former captives, who were accepting no surrender whatever.

Blackie Perales had been one of the latter; he had been found, his clothes in rags and covered with dirt and grease, hiding under a machine in one of the shops back of the dock in which the *Harriet Barne* was being rebuilt. He had tried to claim that he was one of the pirates' prisoners who had eluded the roundup at the beginning of the battle and had been hiding there since. As soon as the real prisoners saw and recognized him, they had fallen upon him and clubbed, kicked and stamped him out of any resemblance to humanity. At that, what he got was probably only a fraction of what he deserved.

The egg breakage had been heavy, and not at all confined to the bad eggs. A third gunboat, the *Banshee*, had been destroyed with all hands during the final attack from outside; in addition, a dozen men had been killed during the fighting in the galleries. Everybody was shocked, except Klem Zareff, who had been in battles before. He was surprised that the casualties had been so light.

At first glance, the spaceport looked like a handsome prize of victory. The docks and workshops were all in good condition; at worst, they only needed cleaning up. There was a collapsium plant, with its own mass-energy converter. There were foundries and machine-shops and forging-shops and a rolling-mill, almost completely robotic. At first, Conn thought that it might be possible to build a hyperdrive ship here, without having to go to Koshchei at all.

Closer examination disabused him of this hope. There was nothing of which the framework of a ship could be built, and no way of producing heavy structural steel. The rolling-mill was good enough to turn out eighth-inch sheet material which when plated with a few micromicrons of collapsium would be as good as a hundred feet of lead against space-radiations, but that was the ship's skin. A ship needed a skeleton, too. The only thing to do was go on with the *Harriet Barne*.

It was sunset before he finished his tour of inspection and let his jeep down in a vehicle hall off the lower gallery outside what had originally been the spaceport officers' club. It was crowded, and a victory celebration seemed to be getting under way. He saw his father with Yves Jacquemont, Sylvie, Tom Brangwyn, and Captain Nichols. Nichols had gotten clean clothes from the pirates' store of loot, and had bathed and shaved. So had Jacquemont, though he had contented himself with trimming his beard. It took him a second or so to recognize the young lady in feminine garb as his erstwhile battle comrade, Sylvie.

"Well, our pay goes on from the day we were captured," Nichols was saying. "My instructions are to resume command of the ship. Tomorrow, they're sending a party out to go over her."

Conn stopped short. "What's this about the ship?"

"Captain Nichols was in screen contact with his company's office in Storisende," Rodney Maxwell said. "They're continuing him in command of her."

"But . . . but we took that ship! We lost three gunboats and about twenty-five men . . ."

"She still belongs to Transcontinent & Overseas," his father said. "That's been the law on stolen property as long as there's been any law."

Of course; he should have known that. Did know it; just didn't think.

"We broke an awful lot of eggs for no omelet; fought a battle for nothing."

"Well, of course, I'm prejudiced," Sylvie said, "but I don't think getting us out of the hands of that bloodthirsty maniac and his cutthroats was nothing."

"Wiping out the Perales gang wasn't nothing, Conn," Tom Brangwyn said. "You got no idea at all how bad things were, the last couple of years."

"I know. I'm sorry." He was ashamed of himself. "But I needed a ship, and now we have no ship at all."

"A ship means something to you?" Yves Jacquemont asked.

"Yes." He told him why. "If we could get to Koshchei, we could build a hypership of our own, and get our brandy and things to markets where we could get a decent price for them."

"I know. I was in and out of Storisende on these owner-captain tramps for a couple of years before I decided to retire and settle here," Jacquemont said. "The profit on a cargo of Poictesme brandy on Terra or Baldur is over a thousand percent."

"Well, don't give up too soon," Nichols advised. "You can't keep the *Harriet Barne*, of course, but you're entitled to prize-money on her, and that ought to buy you something you could build a spaceship out of."

"That's right," Jacquemont said. "Everything else besides the frame can be made here. Look, these pirates burned me out; except for the money I have in the bank, I lost everything, home, business and all. As soon as I can find a place for Sylvie to stay, I'll come back and go to work for your company building a spaceship. And a lot of the men who were working here are farm-tramps and drifters, one job's as good as another as long as they get paid for it. And I know a few good men in Storisende—engineers—who'd be glad for a job, too."

"You think it would be all right with Mother and Flora if Sylvie stayed with us?" Conn asked.

"Of course it would; they'd be glad to have her." Rodney Maxwell turned to Yves Jacquemont. "Let's consider that fixed up. Now, suppose you and I go into Storisende, and . . ."

The Transcontinent & Overseas people arrived at Barathrum Spaceport the next morning; a rear-rank vice-president,
a front-rank legal-eagle, and three engineers. They were
horrified at what they saw. The *Harriet Barne* had been
gutted. Bulkheads and decks had been ripped out and re-
located incomprehensibly; the bridge and the control room
under it were gone; she had been stripped to her framework,
and the whole underside was sheathed in shimmering collapsium.

"Great Ghu!" the vice-president almost howled. "That isn't
our ship!"

"That's the *Harriet Barne*," her captain said. "She looks
a little ragged now, but—"

"You helped these pirates do this to her?"

"If I hadn't, they'd have cut my throat and gotten somebody else to help them. My throat's more valuable to me
than the ship is to you; I can't get anybody to build me a
new one."

"Well, understand," one of the engineers said, "they were
converting her into an interplanetary ship. It wouldn't cost
much to finish the job."

"We need an interplanetary ship like we need a hole in
the head!" The vice-president turned to Rodney Maxwell.
"Just how much prize-money do you think you're entitled
to for this wreck?"

"I wouldn't know; that's up to Sterber, Flynn & Chen-
Wong. Up to the court, if we can settle it any other way."

"You mean you'd litigate about this?" the lawyer demanded,
and began to laugh.

"If we have to. Look, if you people don't want her, sign
her over to Litchfield Exploration & Salvage. But if you do
want her, you'll have to pay for her."

"We'll give you twenty thousand sols," the lawyer said.
"We don't want to be tightfisted. After all, you fought a gang
of pirates and lost some men and a couple of boats; we
have some moral obligation to you. But you'll have to realize
that this ship, in her present state, is practically valueless."

"The collapsium on her is worth twice that, and the engines are worth even more," Jacquemont said. "I worked on them."

The discussion ended there. By midafternoon, Luther Chen-Wong, the junior partner of the law firm, arrived from Storisende with a couple of engineers of his own. Reporters began arriving; both sides were anxious to keep them away from the ship. Conn took care of them, assisted by Sylvie, who had rummaged an even more attractive costume out of what she called the loot-cellar. The reporters all used up a lot of film footage on her. And the Fawzis' Office Gang arrived from Force Command, bitterly critical of the value of the spaceport against its cost in lives and equipment. Brangwyn and Zareff returned to Force Command with them. A Planetary Air Patrol ship arrived and removed the captured pirates. The liberated prisoners were airlifted to Litchfield.

The third day after the battle, Conn and his father and Sylvie and her father flew to Litchfield. To Conn's surprise, Flora greeted him cordially, and Wade Lucas, rather stiffly, congratulated him. Maybe it was as Tom Brangwyn had said; he hadn't been on Poictesme in the last four or five years and didn't know how bad things had gotten. His mother seemed to think he had won the Battle of Barathrum single-handed.

He was even more surprised and gratified that Flora made friends with Sylvie immediately. His mother, however, regarded the engineer's daughter with badly concealed hostility, and seemed to doubt that Sylvie was the kind of girl she wanted her son getting involved with. Outwardly, of course, she was quite gracious.

Rodney Maxwell and Yves Jacquemont flew to Storisende the next morning, both more optimistic about finding a ship than Conn thought the circumstances warranted. Conn stayed at home for the next few days, luxuriating in idleness. He and Sylvie tore down his mother's household robots and built sound-sensors into them, keying them to respond to their names and to a few simple commands, and including recorded-voice responses in a thick Sheshan accent. All the smart people on Terra, he explained, had Sheshan humanoid servants.

His mother was delighted. Robots that would answer when she spoke to them were a lot more companionable. She didn't seem to think, however, that Sylvie's mechanical skills were ladylike accomplishments. Nice girls, Litchfield model, weren't quite so handy with a spot-welder. That was what Conn liked about Sylvie; she was like the girls he'd known at the University.

They were strolling after dinner, down the Mall. The air was sharp and warned that autumn had definitely arrived; the many brilliant stars, almost as bright as the moon of Terra, were coming out in the dusk.

"Conn, this thing about Merlin," she began. "Do you really believe in it? Ever since Dad and I came to Poictesme, I've been hearing about it, but it's just a story, isn't it?"

He was tempted to tell her the truth, and sternly put the temptation behind him.

"Of course there's a Merlin, Sylvie, and it's going to do wonderful things when we find it."

He looked down the starlit Mall ahead of him. Somebody, maybe Lester Dawes and Morgan Gatworth and Lorenzo Menardes, had gotten things finished and cleaned up. The pavement was smooth and unbroken; the litter had vanished.

"It's done wonderful things already, just because people started looking for it," he said. "Some of these days, they're going to realize that they had Merlin all along and didn't know it."

There was a faint humming from somewhere ahead, and he was wondering what it was. Then they came to the long escalators, and he saw that they were running.

"Why, look! They got them fixed! They're running!"

Sylvie grinned at him and squeezed his arm.

"I get you, chum," she said. "Of course there's a Merlin."

Maybe he didn't have to tell her the truth.

When they returned to the house, his mother greeted him:

"Conn, your father's been trying to get you ever since you went out. Call him, right away; Ritz-Gartner Hotel, in Storisende. It's something about a ship."

It look a little time to get his father on-screen. He was excited and happy.

"Hi, Conn; we have one," he said.

"What kind of a ship?"

"You know her. The *Harriet Barne*."

That he hadn't expected. Something off Mothball Row that would have to be flown to Barathrum and torn down and completely rebuilt, but not the one that was there already, partly finished.

"How the dickens did you wangle that?"

"Oh, it was Yves' idea, to start with. He knew about her; the T. & O.'s been losing money on her for years. He said if they had to pay prize-money on her and then either restore her to original condition or finish the job and build a spaceship they didn't want, it would almost bankrupt the company. They got up as high as fifty thousand sols for prize-money and we just laughed at them. So we made a proposition of our own.

"We proposed organizing a new company, subsidiary to both L. E. & S. and T. & O., to engage in interplanetary shipping; both companies to assign their equity in the *Harriet Barne* to the new company, the work of completing her to be done at our spaceport and the labor cost to be shared. This would give us our spaceship, and get T. & O. off the hook all around. Everybody was for it except the president of T. & O. Know anything about him?"

Conn shook his head. His father continued:

"Name's Jethro Sastraman. He could play Scrooge in *Christmas Carol* without any makeup at all. He hasn't had a new idea since he got out of college, and that was while the War was still going on. 'Preposterous; utterly visionary and impractical,' " his father mimicked. "Fortunately, a majority of the big stockholders didn't agree; they finally bullied him into agreeing. We're calling the new company Alpha-Interplanetary, we have an application for charter in, and that'll go through almost automatically."

"Who's going to be the president of this new company?"

"You know him. Character named Rodney Maxwell. Yves is going to be vice-president in charge of operations; he's flying to Barathrum tomorrow or the next day with a gang of technicians we're recruiting. T. & O. are giving us Clyde

Nichols and Mack Vibart, and a lot of men from their shipyard. I'm staying here in Storisende; we're opening an office here. By this time next week, we're all going to wish we'd been born quintuplets."

"And Conn Maxwell, I suppose, will be an influential non-office-holding stockholder?"

"That's right. Just like in L. E. & S."

XII

He found Jerry Rivas and Anse Dawes and a score of workmen making a survey and inventory of the spaceport. Captain Nichols and four of the original crew of the *Harriet Barne*, who had shared his captivity among the pirates, had stayed to take care of the ship. And Fred Karski, with one guncutter and a couple of light airboats, was keeping up a routine guard. All of them had heard about the formation of Alpha-Interplanetary when Conn arrived.

The next day, Yves Jacquemont arrived, accompanied by Mack Vibart, a gang from the T. & O. shipyard, and a dozen engineers and construction men whom he had recruited around Storisende. More workers arrived in the next few days, including a number who had already worked on the ship as slaves of the Perales gang.

It didn't take Conn long to appreciate the problems involved in the conversion. Built to operate only inside planetary atmosphere and gravitation, the *Harriet Barne* was long and narrow, like an old ocean ship; more than anything else, she had originally resembled a huge submarine. Spaceships, either interplanetary or interstellar, were always spherical with a pseudogravity system at the center. This, of course, the *Harriet Barne* lacked.

"Well, are we going to make the whole trip in free fall?" he wanted to know.

"No, we'll use our acceleration for pseudograv halfway, and deceleration the other half," Jacquemont told him. "We'll be in free fall about ten or fifteen hours. What we're going to have to do will be to lift off from Poictesme in the horizontal position the ship was designed for, and then make a ninety-degree turn after we're off-planet, with our lift and our drive working together, just like one of the old rocket ships before the Abbott Drive was developed."

That meant, of course, that the after bulkheads would become decks, and explained a lot of the oddities he had noticed about the conversion job. It meant that everything would have to be mounted on gimbals, everything stowed so as to be secure in either position, and nothing placed where it would be out of reach in either.

Jacquemont and Nichols took charge of the work on the ship herself. Chief Engineer Vibart, with a gang of half-taught, self-taught and untaught helpers, went back to working the engines over, tearing out all the safety devices that were intended to keep the ship inside planetary atmosphere, and arranging the lift engines so that they could be swung into line with the drive engines. There was a lot of cybernetic and robotic equipment, and astrogational equipment, that had to be made from scratch. Conn picked a couple of helpers and went to work on that.

From time to time, he was able to snatch a few minutes to read teleprint papers or listen to audiovisual newscasts from Storisende. He was always disappointed. There was much excitement about the new interplanetary company, but the emphasis was all wrong. People weren't interested in getting hyperships built, or opening the mines and factories on Koshchei, or talking about all the things now in short supply that could be produced there. They were talking about Merlin, and they were all positive, now, that something found at Force Command Duplicate had convinced Litchfield Exploration & Salvage that the giant computor was somewhere off-planet.

Rodney Maxwell flew in from Storisende; he was accompanied by Wade Lucas, who shook hands cordially with Conn.

"Can you spare us Jerry Rivas for a while?" Rodney Maxwell asked.

"Well, ask Yves Jacquemont; he's vice-president in charge of operations. As an influential non-office-holding stockholder, I'd think so. He's only running around helping out here and there."

"We want him to take charge of opening those hospitals you were telling us about. Wade and I are forming a new company, Mainland Medical Materials, Ltd. Going to act as broker for L. E. & S. in getting rid of medical stores. Nobody in the company knows where to sell that stuff or what we ought to get for it."

Wade Lucas began to talk about how desperately some types of drug and some varieties of diagnostic equipment were needed. Conn had it on the tip of his tongue to ask Lucas whether he thought that was a racket, too. Lucas must have read his mind.

"I really didn't understand how much good this would do," he said. "I wouldn't have spoken so forcefully against it if I had. I thought it was nothing but this Merlin thing—"

"Aaagh! Don't talk to me about Merlin!" Conn interrupted. "I have to talk to Kurt Fawzi and that crowd about Merlin till I'm sick of the whole subject."

His father shot him a warning glance; Lucas was looking at him in surprise. He hastened to change the subject:

"I see Len made you a suit out of that material," he said to his father. "And I see you're not bulging the coat out behind with a hip-holster."

"Oh, I stopped carrying a gun; I'm a city man, now. Nobody carries one in Storisende. Won't even be necessary in Litchfield before long. Our new marshal had a regular reign of terror in Tramptown for a few days, and you wouldn't know the place. Wade, here, is acting mayor now."

They went back to talking about the new company. "You're going to have so many companies you won't be able to to keep track of them before long," Conn said.

"Well, I'm doing something about that. A holding company; Trisystem Investments, Ltd.; you're a non-office-holding stockholder in that, too."

Merlin was now a political issue. A bill had been introduced in Parliament to amend the Abandoned Property Act of 867 and nationalize Merlin, when and if discovered and regardless by whom. The support seemed to come from an extremist minority; everybody else, including the Administration, was opposed to it. There was considerable acrimony, however, on the propositions: 1) that Merlin was too important to the prosperity of Poictesme to become a private monopoly; and 2) that Merlin was too important, etc., to become a political football and patronage plum.

It was discovered, after they were half assembled, that the controls for the *Harriet Barne* would only work while she was in a horizontal position. The whole thing had to be torn out and rebuilt. There was also trouble with the air-and-water recycling system. The *City of Nefertiti* came in from Aton for Odin; Rodney Maxwell was almost frantic because they hadn't gotten together a cargo of medical stores from the first hospital to be opened.

"There's all sorts of stuff," he was fuming, by screen. "Stuff that's in short supply anywhere and that we could get good prices for off-planet. Get Federation sols for it, too."

"The *City of Asgard* will be along in six months," Conn said. "You can have a real cargo assembled by then. You can make arrangements in advance to dispose of it on Terra or Baldur or Marduk."

"There are a couple of other companies interested in interplanetary ships now," his father added. "One of them had gotten four old freighters off Mothball Row, and they're tearing them down and cannibalizing them into one spaceship. That work's being done here at Storisende Spaceport. And another company has gotten title to a couple of old office buildings and has a gang at work dismantling them for the structural steel. I think they're going to build a real spaceship."

That wasn't anything to worry about either. The *Harriet Barne* was better than half finished. There was a collapsium plant at Storisende Spaceport, but Yves Jacquemont said it was only half the size of the one at Barathrum; it would be three months before it could produce armor for one, let alone both, ships.

The crackpots were getting into the act, now, too. A spirit medium on the continent of Acaire, to the north, had produced a communication purporting to originate with a deceased Third Force Staff officer, now in the Spirit World. There was considerable detail, all ludicrous to Conn's professional ear. And a fanatic in one of the small towns on the west coast was quoting the Bible, the Koran, and the Bhagavadgita to prove that if Merlin were ever found, Divine vengeance in a spectacular form would fall not only on Poictesme but on the entire Galaxy.

The spaceship that was building at Storisende got into the news; on-screen, it appeared that the work was progressing rapidly. So was the work of demolishing a block of empty buildings to get girders for the second ship, on which work had not yet been started. The one under construction seemed to be of cruciform design, like an old-fashioned pre-contragravity winged airplane. The design puzzled everybody at Barathrum. Yves Jacquemont thought that perhaps there would be decks in the cross-arm which would be used when the ship was running on combined lift and drive.

"Well, till we can get a shipyard going on Koshchei and build some real spaceships, there are going to be some rare-looking objects traveling around the Alpha System. I wonder what the next one's going to look like—a flying skyscraper?" Conn said.

"What I wonder," Yves Jacquemont replied, "is where all the old interplanetary ships got to. There must have been hundreds of them running back and forth from here to Janicot and Koshchei and Jurgen and Horvendile during the War. They must have gone somewhere."

"Couldn't they all have been fitted with Dillingham hyperdrive engines and used in the evacuation?"

"Possible. But the average interplanetary ship isn't very big; five hundred to seven-fifty feet in diameter. One of those things couldn't carry more than a couple of hundred people, after you put in all the supplies and the hydroponic tanks and carniculture vats and so on for a four- to six-month voyage. I can't see the economy of altering anything that small for interstellar work. Why, the smallest of these tramp freighters that come in here will run about fifteen hundred feet."

They didn't just disintegrate when peace broke out, that was for sure. And there certainly weren't any of them left on Poictesme. He puzzled over it briefly, then shoved it aside. He had more important things to think about.

In his spare time he was studying, along with his other work, everything he could find on Koshchei, with an intensity he had not given to anything since cramming for examinations at the University. There was a lot of it.

The fourth planet of Alpha Gartner was older than Poictesme; geologists claimed that it was the oldest thing, the sun excepted, in the system, and astrophysicists were far from convinced that it hadn't been captured from either Beta or Gamma when the three stars had been much closer together. It had certainly been formed at a much higher temperature than Janicot or Poictesme or Jurgen or Horvendile. For better than a billion years, it had been molten-hot, and it had lost most of its lighter elements in gaseous form along with its primary atmosphere, leaving little to form a light-rock crust. All that had remained had been a core of almost pure iron and a mantle that was mostly high-grade iron ore.

The same process had gone on, as it cooled, as on any Terra-size planet. After the surface had started to congeal, gases, mostly carbon dioxide and water vapor, had come up to form a secondary atmosphere, the water vapor forming a cloud envelope, condensing, and sending down rain that returned immediately as steam. Solar radiations and electric discharges broke some of that into oxygen and hydrogen; most of the hydrogen escaped into space. Finally, the surface cooled further and the rain no longer steamed off.

The whole planet started to rust. It had been rusting, slowly, for the billion or so years that had followed, and

102

almost all the free oxygen had become locked in iron oxide. The air was almost pure carbon dioxide. It would have been different if life had ever appeared on Koshchei, but apparently the right amino acids never assembled. Some attempts had been made to introduce vegetation after the colonization of Poictesme, but they had all failed.

Men went to Koshchei; they worked out of doors in oxygen helmets, and lived in airtight domes and generated their own oxygen. There had been mines, and smelters, and blast furnaces and steel mills. And there had been shipyards, where hyperships up to three thousand feet had been built. They had all been abandoned when the War had ended; they were waiting there, on an empty, lifeless planet. Some of them had been built by the Third Fleet-Army Force during the War; most of them dated back almost a century before that, to the original industrial boom. All of them could be claimed under the Abandoned Property Act of 867, since all had been taken over by the Federation, and the original owners, or their heirs, compensated.

And there was the matter of selecting a crew. As an influential non-office-holding stockholder in all the companies involved, Conn Maxwell, of course, would represent them. He would also serve as astrogator. Clyde Nichols would command the ship in atmosphere, and act as first mate in space. Mack Vibart would be chief engineer at all times. Yves Jacquemont would be first officer under Nichols, and captain outside atmosphere. They had three real space crewmen, named Roddell, Youtsko and O'Keefe, who had been in Storisende jail as a result of a riotous binge when their ship had lifted out, six months before. The rest of the company—Jerry Rivas, Anse Dawes, Charley Gatworth, Mohammed Matsui, and four other engineers, Ludvyckson, Gomez, Karanja and Retief—rated as ordinary spacemen for the trip, and would do most of the exploration work after landing.

They got the controls put up; they would work in either position. The engines were lifted in and placed. Conn finished the robo-pilot and the astrogational computers and saw them installed. The air-and-water recycling system went in. The collapsium armor went on. In the news-screen, they saw the spaceship at Storisende still far from half finished, with swarms of heavy-duty lifters and contragravity machiners around it, and a set of landing-stands, on which the second ship was to be built, in the process of construction.

A tramp hyperspace freighter landed at Storisende, the *Andromeda*, five months from Terra, with a cargo of general merchandise. Rodney Maxwell and Wade Lucas had assembled a cargo of medicines and hospital equipment which they thought could be sold profitably. They began dickering with the owner-captain of the hypership.

A farm-tramp down in the tobacco country to the south, evidently ignorant that the former commander of the Third Force was still alive, had proclaimed himself to be the reincarnation of Foxx Travis and was forbidding everybody, on pain of court-martial and firing squad, from meddling with Merlin. And an evangelist in the west was declaring that Merlin was really Satan in mechanical shape.

The *Harriet Barne* was finished. The first test, lifting her to three hundred miles, turning her bow-up, and taking her another thousand miles, had been a success. They brought her back and set her down in the middle of the crater, and began getting the supplies aboard. Kurt Fawzi, Klem Zareff, Judge Ledue, Franz Veltrin and the others flew over from Force Comand. Sylvie Jacquemont came from Litchfield, and so did Wade Lucas, Morgan Gatworth, Lester Dawes, Lorenzo Menardes and a number of others. Neither Conn's mother nor sister came.

"I don't know what's the matter with those two," Sylvie told him. "They always seem to be scrapping with each other now, and the only thing they can agree on is that you and your father ought to stop whatever you're doing, right away. Your mother can't adjust to your father being a big Storisende businessman, and she says he'll lose every centisol he has and both of you will probably go to jail, and then she's afraid you will find Merlin, and Flora's sure you and your father are swindling everybody on the planet."

"Sylvie, I had no idea things would be like that," he told

her contritely. "I wish I hadn't suggested that you stay there, now."

"Oh, it isn't so bad, so far. Your mother and I get along all right when Flora isn't there, and Flora and I get along when your mother isn't around. Mealtimes aren't much fun, though."

His father came out from Storisende, looked the ship over, and seemed relieved.

"I'm glad you're ready to get off," he said. "You know this hyperspace freighter, the *Andromeda?* Some private group in Storisende has chartered her. She's loading supplies now. I have a private detective agency, Barton-Massarra, trying to find out where's she's going. I think you'd better get this ship off, right away."

"We have everything aboard, all the supplies and everything," Jacquemont told him. "We can lift off tonight."

XIII

The ship lurched slightly. In the outside screens, the lights around, the crowd that was waving good-bye, and the floor of the crater began receding. The sound pickups were full of cheering, and the boom of a big gun at one of the top batteries, and the recorded and amplified music of a band playing the traditional "Spacemen's Hymn."

"It's been a long time since I heard that played in earnest," Jacquemont said. "Well, we're off to see the Wizard."

The lights dwindled and merged into a tiny circle in the darkness of the crater. The music died away; the cannon shots became a faint throbbing. Finally, there was silence, and only the stars above and the dark land and the starlit sea below. After a long while a sunset glow, six hours past on Barathrum, appeared in the west, behind the now appreciable curvature of the planet.

"Stand by for shift to vertical," Captain Nichols called, his voice echoing from PA-outlets through the ship.

"Ready for shift, Captain Nichols," Jacquemont reported from the duplicate-control panel.

Conn went to the after bulkhead, leaning his back against it. "Ready here, Captain," he said.

Other voices took it up. Lights winked on the control panels.

"Shifting over," Nichols said. "Your ship now, Captain Jacquemont."

"Thank you, Mr. Nichols."

The deck began to tilt, and then he was lying on his back, his feet against the side of the control room, which had altered its shape and dimensions. There was a jar as the drive went on in line with the new direction of the lift and the ship began accelerating. He got to his feet, and he and Charley Gatworth went to the astrogational computer and began checking the data and setting the course for the point in space at which Koshchei would be in a hundred and sixty hours.

"Course set, Captain," he reported to Jacquemont, after a while.

A couple of lights winked on the control panel. There was nothing more to do but watch Poictesme dwindle behind, and listen to the newscasts, and take turns talking to friends on the planet.

They approached the halfway point; the acceleration rate decreased, and the gravity indicator dropped, little by little. Everybody was enjoying the new sense of lightness, romping and skylarking like newly landed tourists on Luna. It was fun, as long as they landed on their feet at each jump, and the food and liquids stayed on plates and in glasses and cups. Yves Jacquemont began posting signs in conspicuous places:

WEIGHT IS WHAT YOU LIFT, MASS IS WHAT HURTS
WHEN IT HITS YOU.
WEIGHT DEPENDS ON GRAVITY; MASS IS ALWAYS CONSTANT.

His father came on-screen from his office in Storisende. By then, there was a 30-second time lag in communication between the ship and Poictesme.

"My private detectives found out about the *Andromeda*," he said. "She's going to Panurge, in the Gamma System. They have a couple of computermen with them, one they hired from the Stock Exchange, and one they practically shanghaied away from the Government. And some of the people who chartered the ship are members of a family that were interested in a positronic-equipment plant on Panurge at the time of the War."

"That's all right, then; we don't need to worry about that any more. They're just hunting for Merlin."

Some of his companions were looking at him curiously. A little later, Piet Ludvyckson, the electromagnetics engineer, said: "I thought you were looking for Merlin, Conn."

"Not on Koschchei. We're looking for something to build a hypership out of. If I had Merlin in my hip pocket right now, I'd trade it for one good ship like the *City of Asgard* or the *City of Nefertiti*, and give a keg of brandy and a box of cigars to boot. If we had a ship of our own, we'd be selling lots of both, and not for Storisende Spaceport prices, either."

"But don't you think Merlin's important?" Charley Gatworth, who had overheard him, asked.

"Sure. If we find Merlin, we can run it for President. It would make a better one than Jake Vyckhoven."

He let it go at that. Plenty of opportunities later to expand the theme.

The gravitation gauge dropped to zero. Now they were in free fall, and it lasted twice as long as Yves Jacquemont had predicted. There were a few misadventures, none serious and most of them comic— For example, when Jerry Rivas opened a bottle of beer, everybody was chasing the amber globules and catching them in cups, and those who were splashed were glad it hadn't been hot coffee.

They made their second, 180-degree turnover while weightless. Then they began decelerating and approached Koshchei stern-on, and the gravity gauge began climbing slowly up again, and things began staying put, and they were walking instead of floating. Koshchei grew larger and larger ahead; the polar icecaps, and the faint dappling of clouds, and the dark wiggling lines on the otherwise uniform red-brown surface which were mountain ranges became visible. Finally they began to see, first with the telescopic screens and then without magnification, the little dots and specks that were cities and industrial centers.

Then they were in atmosphere, and Jacquemont made the final shift, to horizontal position, and turned the ship over to Nichols.

For a moment, the scout-boat tumbled away from the ship and Conn was back in free fall. Then he got on the lift-and-drive and steadied it, and pressed the trigger button, firing a green smoke bomb. Beside him, Yves Jacquemont put on the radio and the screen pickups. He could see the ship circling far above, and the manipulator-boat, with its claw-arms and grapples, breaking away from it. Then he looked down on the endless desert of iron oxide that stretched in all directions to the horizon, until he saw a spot, optically the size of a five-centisol piece, that was the shipbuilding city of Port Carpenter. He turned the boat toward it, firing four more green smokes at three-second intervals. The manipulator-boat started to follow, and the *Harriet Barne*, now a distant speck in the sky, began coming closer.

Below, as he cut speed and altitude, he could see the pock-marks of open-pit mines and the glint of sunlight on bright metal and armor-glass roofs, the blunt conical stacks of nuclear furnaces and the twisted slag-flows, like the ancient lava-flows of Barathrum. And, he reflected, he was an influential non-office-holding stockholder in every bit of it, as soon as they could screen Storisende and get claims filed.

A high tower rose out of the middle of Port Carpenter, with a glass-domed mushroom top. That would be the telecast station; the administrative buildings were directly below it and around its base. He came in slowly over the city, above a spaceport with its empty landing pits in a double circle around a traffic-control building, and airship docks and warehouses beyond. More steel mills. Factories, either hemispherical domes or long buildings with rounded tops. Ship-construction yards and docks; for the most part, these were empty, but on some of them the landing-stands of spaceships, like eight- and ten-legged spiders, waiting for forty years for hulls to be built on them. A few spherical skeletons of ships, a few with some of the outer skin on. It wasn't until he was passing close to them that he realized how huge they were. And stacks of material—sheet steel, deckplate, girders—and contragravity lifters and construction machines, all left on jobs that were never finished, the bright rustless metal dulled by forty years of rain and windblown red dust. They must have been working here to the very last, and then, when the evacuation elsewhere was completed, they had dropped whatever they were doing, piled into such ships as were completed, and lifted away.

The mushroom-topped tower rose from the middle of a circular building piled level on level, almost half a mile across. He circled over it, saw an airship dock, and called the *Harriet Barne* while Jacquemont talked to Jerry Rivas, piloting the manipulator-boat. Rivas came in and joined them in the air; they hovered over the dock and helped the ship down when she came in, nudging her into place.

By the time Conn and Jacquemont and Rivas and Anse Dawes and Roddell and Youtsko and Karanja were out on the dock in oxygen helmets, the ship's airlock was opening and Nichols and Vibart and the others were coming out, towing a couple of small lifters loaded with equipment.

The airlocked door into the building, at the end of the dock, was closed; when somebody pulled the handle, it refused to open. That meant it was powered from the central power plant, wherever that was. There was a plug socket beside it, with the required voltage marked over it. They used an extension line from a power unit on one of the lifters to get it open, and did the same with the inner door; when it was open, they passed into a dim room that stretched away ahead of them and on either side.

It looked like a freight-shipping room; there were a few

piles of boxes and cases here and there, and a litter of packing material everywhere. A long counter-desk, and a bank of robo-clerks behind it. According to the air-analyzer, the oxygen content inside was safely high. They all pulled off their fishbowl helmets and slung them.

"Well, we can bunk inside here tonight," somebody said. "It won't be so crowded here."

"We'll bunk here after we find the power plant and get the ventilator fans going," Jacquemont said.

Anse Dawes held up the cigarette he had lighted; that was all the air-analyzer he needed.

"That looks like enough oxygen," he said.

"Yes, it makes its own ventilation; convection," Jacquemont said. "But you go to sleep in here, and you'll smother in a big puddle of your own exhaled CO_2. Just watch what the smoke from that cigarette's doing."

The smoke was hanging motionless a few inches from the hot ash on the end of the cigarette.

"We'll have to find the power plant, then," Matsui, the power-engineer said. "Down at the bottom and in the middle, I suppose, and anybody's guess how deep this place goes."

"We'll find plans of the building," Jerry Rivas said. "Any big dig I've ever been on, you could always find plans. The troubleshooters always had them; security officer, and maintenance engineer."

There were inside-use vehicles in the big room; they loaded what they had with them onto a couple of freight-skids and piled on, starting down a passage toward the center of the building. The passageways were well marked with direction-signs, and they found the administrative area at the top and center, around the base of the telecast-tower. The security offices, from which police, military guard, fire protection and other emergency services were handled, had a fine set of plans and maps, not only for the building itself but for everything else in Port Carpenter. The power plant, as Matsui had surmised, was at the very bottom, directly below.

The only trouble, after they found it, was that it was completely dead. The reactors wouldn't react, the converters wouldn't convert, and no matter how many switches they shoved in, there was no power output. The inside teleme-tered equipment, of course, was self-powered. Some of them were dead, too, but from those which still worked Mo-hammed Matsui got a uniformly disheartening story.

"You know what happened?" he said. "When this gang bugged out, back in 854, they left the power on. Now the conversion mass is all gone, and the plutonium's all spent. We'll have to find more plutonium, and tear this whole thing down and refuel it, and repack the mass-conversion cham-bers—provided nothing's eaten holes in itself after the mass inside was all converted."

"How long will it take?" Conn asked.

"If we can find plutonium, and if we can find robots to do the work inside, and if there's been no structural damage, and if we keep at it—a couple of days."

"All right; let's get at it. I don't know where we'll find shipyards like these anywhere else, and if we do, things'll probably be as bad there. We came here to fix things up and start them, didn't we?"

XIV

IT DIDN'T take as long as Mohammed Matsui expected. They found the fissionables magazine, and in it plenty of pluton-ium, each sub-critical slug in a five-hundred-pound collap-sium canister. There were repair-robots, and they only had to replace the cartridges in the power units of three of them. They sent them inside the collapsium-shielded death-to-people area—transmitter robots, to relay what the others picked up through receptors wire-connected with the out-side; foremen-robots, globes a yard in diameter covered with horns and spikes like old-fashioned ocean-navy mines; worker-robots, in a variety of shapes, but mostly looking like many-clawed crabs.

Neither the converter nor the reactor had sustained any damage while the fissionables were burning out. So the robots began tearing out reactor-elements, and removing plutonium slugs no longer capable of sustaining chain reaction but still dangerously radioactive. Nuclear reactors had become simpler and easier to service since the First Day of the Year Zero, when Enrico Fermi put the first one into operation, but the principles remained the same. Work was less back-breaking and muscle-straining, but it called for intense concentration on screens and meters and buttons that was no less exhausting.

The air around them began to grow foul. Finally, the air-analyzer squawked and flashed red lights to signal that the oxygen had dropped below the safety margin. They had no mobile fan equipment, or time to hunt any; they put on their fishbowl helmets and went back to work. After twelve hours, with a few short breaks, they had the reactors going. Jerry Rivas and a couple of others took a heavy-duty lifter and went looking for conversion mass; they brought back a couple of tons of scrap-iron and fed it to the converters. A few seconds after it was in, the pilot lights began coming on all over the panels. They took two more hours to get the oxygen-separator and the ventilator fans going, and for good measure they started the water pumps and the heating system. Then they all went outside to the ship to sleep. The sun was just coming up.

It was sunset when they rose and returned to the building. The airlocks opened at a touch on the operating handles. Inside, the air was fresh and sweet, the temperature was a pleasantly uniform 75 degrees Fahrenheit, the fans were humming softly, and there was running hot and cold water everywhere.

Jerry Rivas, Anse Dawes, and the three tramp freighter fo'c'sle hands took lifters and equipment and went off foraging. The rest of them went to the communications center to get the telecast station, the radio beacon, and the inside-screen system into operation. There were a good many things that had to be turned on manually, and more things that had been left on, forty years ago, and now had to be repowered or replaced. They worked at it most of the night; before morning, almost everything was working, and they were sending a signal across twenty-eight million miles to Storisende, on Poictesme.

It was late evening, Storisende time, but Rodney Maxwell, who must have been camping beside his own screen, came on at once, which is to say five and a half minutes later.

"Well, I see you got in somewhere. Where are you, and how is everything?"

Then he picked up a cigar out of an ashtray in front of him and lit it, waiting.

"Port Carpenter; we're in the main administration building," Conn told him. He talked for a while about what they had found and done since their arrival. "Have you an extra viewscreen, fitted for recording?" he asked.

Five and a half minutes later, his father nodded. "Yes, right here." He leaned forward and away from the communication screen in front of him. "I have it on." He gave the wave-length combination. "Ready to receive."

"This is about all we have, now. Views we took coming in, from the ship and a scout-boat." He started transmitting them. "We haven't sent in any claims yet. I wasn't sure whether I should make them for Alpha-Interplanetary, or Litchfield Exploration & Salvage."

"Don't bother sending in anything to the Claims Office," his father said. "Send anything you want to claim in here to me, and I'll have Sterber, Flynn & Chen-Wong file them. They'll be made for a new company we're organizing."

"What? Another one?"

His father nodded, grinning. "Koshchei Exploitation & Development; we've made application already. We can't claim exclusive rights to the whole planet, like the old interstellar exploration companies did before the War, but since you're the only people on the planet, we can come pretty close to it by detail." He was looking to one side, at the other screen. "Great Ghu, Conn! This place of yours all together beats everything I ever dug, Force Command and Barathrum Spaceport included. How big would you say it is? More than ten miles in radius?"

"About five or six. Ten or twelve miles across."

"That's all right, then. We'll just claim the building you're in, now, and the usual ten-mile radius, the same as at Force Command. We'll claim the place as soon as the company's chartered; in the meantime, send in everything else you can get views of."

They set up a regular radio-and-screen watch after that. Charley Gatworth and Piet Ludvyckson, both of whom were studying astrogation in hopes of qualifying as space officers after they had a real spaceship, elected themselves to that duty; it gave them plenty of time for study. Jerry Rivas and Anse Dawes, with whomever they could find to help them, were making a systematic search. They looked first of all for foodstuffs, and found enough in the storerooms of three restaurants on the executive level to feed their own party in gourmet style for a year, and enough in the main storerooms to provision an army. They even found refrigerators and freeze-bins full of meat and vegetables fresh after forty years. That surprised everybody, for the power units had gone dead long ago. Then it was noticed that they were covered with collapsium. Anything that would stop cosmic rays was a hundred percent efficient as a heat insulator.

Coming in, the first day, Conn had seen an almost completed hypership bulking above the domes and roofs of Port Carpenter in the distance. He saw it again on screen from a pickup atop the central tower. As soon as the party was comfortably settled in the executive apartments on the upper levels, he and Yves Jacquemont and Mack Vibart and Schalk Retief, the construction engineer, found an aircar in one of the hangars and went to have a closer look at her.

She had all her collapsium on, except for a hundred-foot circle at the top and a number of rectangular openings around the sides. Yves Jacquemont said that would be where the airlocks would go.

"They always put them on last. But don't be surprised at anything you find or don't find inside. As soon as the skele-

114

ton's up they put the armor on, and then build the rest of the ship out from the middle. It might be slower getting material in through the airlock openings, but it holds things together while they're working."

They put on the car's lights, lifted to the top, and let down through the upper opening. It was like entering a huge globular spider's web, globe within globe of interlaced girders and struts and braces, extending from the center to the outer shell. Even the spider was home—a three-hundred-foot ball of collapsium, looking tiny at the very middle.

"Why, this isn't a ship!" Vibart cried in disgust. "This is just the outside of a ship. They haven't done a thing inside."

"Oh, yes, they have," Jacquemont contradicted, aiming a spotlight toward the shimmering ball in the middle. "They have all the engines in—Abbott lift-and-drive, Dillingham hyperdrives, pseudograv, power reactors, converters, everything. They wouldn't have put on the shielding if they hadn't. They did that as soon as they had the outside armor on."

"Wonder why they didn't finish her, if they got that far," Retief said.

"They didn't need her. They'd had it; they wanted to go home."

"Well, we're not going to finish her, not with any fifteen men," Retief said. "One man has only two hands, two feet and one brain; he can only handle so much robo-equipment at a time."

"I never expected we'd build a ship ourselves," Conn said. "We came to look the place over and get a few claims staked. When we've done that, we'll go back and get a real gang together."

"I don't know where you'll find them," Jacquemont commented. "We'll need a couple of hundred, and they ought all to be graduate engineers. We can't do this job with farm-tramps."

"You made some good shipyard men out of farm-tramps on Barathrum."

"And what'll you do for supervisors?"

"You're one. General superintendent. Mack, you and Schalk are a couple of others. You just keep a day ahead of your men in learning the job, you'll do all right."

Vibart turned to Jacquemont. "You know, Yves, he'll do it," he said. "He doesn't know how impossible this is, and when we try to tell him, he won't believe us. You can't stop a guy like that. All right, Conn; deal me in."

"I won't let anybody be any crazier than I am," Jacquemont declared, and then looked around the vastness of the empty ship with its lacework of steel. "All you need is about ten million square feet of decks and bulkheads, and air-and-water system, hydroponic tanks and carniculture vats, astrogation and robo-pilot equipment, about which I know very little, a hyperspace pilot system, about which I know nothing at all . . . Conn, why don't you just build a new Merlin? It would be simpler."

"I don't want a new Merlin. I'm not even interested in the original Merlin. This is what I want, right here."

He told his father, by screen, about the ship. "I believe we can finish her, but not with the gang that's here. We'll need a couple of hundred men. Now, with the supplies we've found, we can stay here indefinitely. Should we do more exploring and claim some more of these places, or should we come home right away and start recruiting, and then come back with a large party, start work on the ship, and explore and make further claims as we have time?" he asked.

"Better come back as soon as possible. Just explore Port Carpenter, find out what's going to be needed to finish the ship and what facilities you have to produce it, and get things cleaned up a little so that you can start work as soon as you have people to do it. I'm organizing another company—don't laugh, now; I've only started promotioneering—which I think we will call Trisystem & Interstellar Spacelines. Get me all the views you can of the ship herself and of the steel mills and that sort of thing that will produce material for finishing her; I want to use them in promotion. By the way, has she a name?"

"Only a shipyard construction number."

"Then suppose you call her *Ouroboros,* after Genji Gartner's old ship, the one that discovered the Trisystem."

"*Ouroboros II;* that's fine. Will do."

"Good. I'll have Sterber, Flynn & Chen-Wong make application for a charter right away. We'll have to make Alpha-Interplanetary one of the stockholding companies, and also Koschchei Exploitation & Development, and, of course, Litchfield Exploration & Salvage. . . ."

It was a pity there really wasn't a Merlin. If this kept on nothing else would be able to figure out who owned how much stock in what.

They found the on-the-job engineering office for the ship in a small dome half a mile from the construction dock. Yves Jacquemont and Mack Vibart and Schalk Retief moved in and buried themselves to the ears in specifications and blueprints. The others formed into parties of three or four, and began looking about production facilities for material. There was a steel mill a mile from the construction site; it was almost fully robotic. Iron ore went in at one end, and finished sheet steel and girders and deck plates came out at the other, and a dozen men could handle the whole thing. There was a collapsium plant; there were machine-shops and forging-shops. Every time they finished inspecting one, Yves Jacquemont would have a list of half a dozen more plants that he wanted found and examined yesterday morning at the latest.

Some of them were in a frightful mess; work had been suspended and everybody had gone away leaving everything as it was. Some were in perfect order, ready to go into operation again as soon as power was put on. It had depended, apparently, upon the personal character of whoever had been in charge in the end. The nuclear-electric power unit plant was in the latter class. The man in charge of it evidently hadn't believed in leaving messes behind, even if he didn't expect to come back.

It was built in the shape of a T. One side of the crossstroke contained the cartridge-case plant, where presses formed sheet-steel cylinders, some as small as a round of pistol ammunition and some the size of ten-gallon kegs. They moved toward the center on a production line, finally reaching a matter-collapser where they were plated with collapsium. From the other side, radioactive isotopes, mostly reactor-waste, came in through evacuated and collapsium-shielded chambers, were sorted, and finally, where the cross-arm of the T joined the downstroke, packed in the collapsium cases. The production line continued at right angles down the long building in which the apparatus which converted nuclear energy to electric current was assembled and packed; at the end, the finished power cartridges came off, big ones for heavy machines and tiny ones for things like hand tools and pocket lighters and razors. There were stacks of them, in all sizes, loaded on skids and ready to move out. Except for the minute and unavoidable leakage of current, they were as good as the day they were assembled, and would be for another century.

Like almost everything else, the power-cartridge plant was airtight and had its own oxygen-generator. The air-analyzer reported the oxygen insufficient to support life. That was understandable; there were a lot of furnaces which had evidently been hot when the power was cut off; they had burned up the oxygen before cooling. They put on their oxygen equipment when they got out of the car.

"I'll go back and have a look at the power plant," Matsui said. "If it's like the rest of this place, it'll be ready to go as soon as the reactors are started. I wish everybody here had left things like this."

"Well, we'll have to check everything to make sure nothing was left on when the main power was cut," Conn said. "Don't do anything back there till we give you the go-ahead."

Matsui nodded and set off on foot along the broad aisle in the middle. Conn looked around in the dim light that filtered through the dusty glass overhead. On either side of the central aisle were two production lines; between each pair, at intervals, stood massive machines which evidently fabricated parts for the power cartridges. Over them, and over the machines directly involved in production, were receptor aerials, all oriented toward a stubby tower, twenty feet thick and fifty in height, topped by a hemispherical dome.

"That'll be the control tower for all the machinery in here," he decided. "Anse, suppose you and I go take a look at it."

"We'll take a look at the machines," Rivas said. "Clyde, you and I can work back on the right and then come down on the other side. You know anything about this stuff?"

"Me? Nifflheim, no," Nichols said. "I know a robo-control when I see one, and I know whether it's set to receive or not."

There was a self-powered lift inside the control tower. Conn and Anse rode it to the top and got out, Anse snapping on his flashlight. It was dark in the dome at the top; instead of windows there were viewscreens all around it. Five men had worked here; at least, there were four chairs at four intricate control panels, one for each of the four production lines, and a fifth chair in front of a number of communication screens. There was a heavy-duty power unit, turned off. Conn threw the switch. Lights came on inside, and the outside viewscreens lit.

They were examining the control-panels when Conn's belt radio buzzed. He plugged it in on his helmet. It was Mohammed Matsui.

"There's one big power plant back here," the engineer said. "Right in the middle. It only powers what's in front of it. There must be another one in either wing, for the isotope plant and the cartridge-case plant. I'll go look at them. But the power's been cut off from the machines in the main building. There's four big switches, one for each production line—"

He was interrupted by a shout, almost a shriek, from somewhere. It sounded like Jerry Rivas. A moment later, Rivas was clamoring:

"Conn! What did you turn on? Turn it off, right away!"

Anse jumped to the switch, pulling it with one hand and getting on his flashlight with the other. The lights went out and the screens went dark.

"It's off."

"The dickens it is!" Rivas disputed. "There are a couple of big supervisor-robots circling around, and a flock of workers. . . ."

At the same time, Clyde Nichols began cursing. Or maybe he was praying; it was hard to be certain.

"But we pulled the switch. It was only the lights and viewscreens in here, anyhow."

"It didn't do any good. Pull another one."

Matsui, back at the power plant, was wanting to know what was wrong. Captain Nichols stopped cursing—or praying?—and said, "Mutiny, that's what! The robots have turned on us!"

He knew what had happened, or was almost sure he did. A radio impulse had gone out, somehow, from the control tower. Something they hadn't checked, that had been left on. There was just enough current-leakage from the units in the robots to keep the receptors active for forty years. The supervisor-robots had gone active, and they had activated the rest. Once on, cutting the current from the control tower wouldn't turn them off again.

"Put the switch in again, Anse; the damage is done and you won't make it any worse."

When the screens came on, he looked around from one to another. The two supervisors, big ovoid things like the small round ones they had used in repairing the power reactors the first day, were circling aimlessly near the roof, one clockwise and the other counterclockwise, dodging obstructions and getting politely out of each other's way. At lower altitude, a dozen assorted worker-robots were moving about, and more were emerging from cells at the end of the building. Sweepers, with rotary brooms and rakes, crablike all-purpose handling robots, a couple of vacuum-cleaning robots, each with a flexible funnel-tipped proboscis and a bulging dust-sack. One thing, a sort of special job designed to get into otherwise inaccessible places, had a twenty-foot, many-jointed, claw-tipped arm in front. It passed by and slightly over the tower, saw Clyde Nichols, and swooped toward him. With a howl, Nichols dived under one of the large machines between two production lines. A pistol went off a couple of times. That would be Jerry Rivas. Nobody else bothered with a gun on Koshchei, but he carried one as some people carry umbrellas, whether he expected to need it or not and because he would feel lost without it.

That he took in at one glance. Then he was looking at the control panels. The switches and buttons were all marked for machine-control in different steps of power-unit production. That was all for the big stuff, powered centrally. There weren't any controls for lifters or conveyers or other mobile equipment. Evidently they were handled out in the shop, from mobile control-vehicles. He did find, on the communication-screen panel, a lot of things that had been left on. He snapped them off, one after another, snapping them on when a screen went dark. There were fifteen or twenty robots, some rather large, in the air or moving on the floor by now.

"We can't do anything here," he told Anse. "These are the shop-cleaning robots. They were the last things used here when the place closed down, and the two supervisors were probably controlled from a vehicle, and it's anybody's guess where that is now. When you threw that switch, it sent out an impulse that activated them. They're running their instruction-tapes, and putting the others through all their tricks."

Three more shots went off. Jerry Rivas was shouting: "Hey, whattaya know! I killed one of the buggers!"

There were any number of ways in which a work-robot could be shot out of commission with a pistol. All of them would be by the purest of pure luck. The next time we go into a place like this, Conn thought, we take a couple of bazookas along.

"Turn everything off and let's go. See what we can do outside."

Anse put on his flashlight and pulled the switch. They got into the lift and rode down, going outside. As soon as they emerged, they saw a rectangular object fifteen feet long settle over their aircar, let down half a dozen clawed arms, and pick it up, flying away with it. It had taped instructions to remove anything that didn't belong in the aisleway; it probably asked the supervisor about the aircar, and the supervisor didn't return an inhibitory signal, so it went ahead. Conn and Anse both shouted at it, knowing perfectly well that shouting was futile. Then they were running for their lives with one of the crablike all-purpose jobs after them. They dived under the slightly raised bed of a long belt-conveyer and crawled. Jerry Rivas fired another shot, somewhere.

The robots themselves were having troubles. They had done all the work they were supposed to do; now the supervisors were insisting that they do it over again. Uncomplainingly, they swept and raked and vacuum-cleaned where they had vacuum-cleaned and raked and swept forty years ago. The scrap-pickers, having picked all the scrap, were going over the same places and finding nothing, and then getting deflected and gathering a lot of things not definable as scrap, and then circling around, darting away from one another in obedience to their radar-operated evasion-systems, and trying to get to the outside scrap pile, and finding that the doors wouldn't open because the door openers weren't turned on, and finally dumping what they were carrying when the supervisors gave them no instructions.

One of them seemed to have dumped something close to where Clyde Nichols was hiding; if his language had been a little stronger, it would have burned out Conn's radio. Their own immediate vicinity being for the moment clear of flying robots, Conn and Anse rolled from under the conveyer and legged it between the two production lines. Immediately, three of the crablike all-purpose handling-robots saw them, if that was the word for it, and came dashing for them, followed by a thing that was mostly dump-lifter; it was banging its bin-lid up and down angrily. About fifty yards ahead, Jerry Rivas stepped from behind a machine and fired; one of the handling-robots flashed green from underneath, went off contragravity, and came down with a crash. Immediately, like wolves on a wounded companion, the other two pounced upon it, dragging and pulling against each other. That was a hunk of junk; their orders were to remove it.

The mobile trash-bin went zooming up to the ceiling, reversed within twenty feet of it and came circling back to the ground, to go zooming up again. It had gone crazy, literally. It had been getting too many contradictory orders from its supervisor, and its circuits were overloaded and its relays jammed. Rats in mazes and human-type people in financial difficulties go psychotic in very much the same way.

The two surviving all-purpose robots were also headed for a padded repair shop. They had come close enough to each other to activate their anticollision safeties. Immediately, they flew apart. Then their order to pick up that big piece of junk took over, and they started forward again, to be bounced apart as soon as they were within five feet of one another. If left alone, their power units would run down in a year or so; until then, they would keep on trying.

Soulless intelligences, indeed! Then it occurred to him that for the past however-long-it-had-been he hadn't heard from Mohammed Matsui. He jiggled his radio.

"Ham, where are you? Are you still alive?"

"I'm back at the power plant," Matsui said exasperatedly. "There's a big thing circling around here; every time I stick my head out, he makes a dive at me. I didn't know robots would attack people."

"They don't. He just thinks you're some more trash he's been told to gather up."

Matsui was indignant. Conn laughed.

"On the level, Ham. He has photoelectric vision, and a picture of what that aisle is supposed to look like. When you get out in it, he knows you don't belong there and tries to grab you."

"Hey, there's a lot of junk in here in a couple of baskets at the converter. Say I chuck one out to him; what would he do?"

"Grab it and take it away, like he's taped to do."

"Okay; wait a minute."

They couldn't see the archway to the power plant, or even the robot that had Matsui penned up, but after a few minutes they saw it soaring away, clutching a big wire basket full of broken boxes and other rubbish. It headed for the mutually repelling swarm of robots around the door that wouldn't open for them. Conn and Anse and Jerry ran toward the rear, joined by Clyde Nichols, who popped up from behind a pile of spools of electric wire. They made it just before the coffin-shaped thing that had carried off the aircar came over to investigate.

"You want to be careful back there," Matsui told them, as they started toward the temporary safety of the power plant. "All the reactor-repair robots are there; don't get *them* on the warpath next."

Of course! There were always repair-robots at a power plant, to go into places no human could enter and live. Behind the collapsium shielding, they wouldn't have been activated.

"Let's have a look at them. What kind?"

"Standard reactor-servicers; the same we used at the administration center."

Matsui opened the door, and they went into the power plant. Conn and Matsui put on the service-power and activated the two supervisors; they, in turn, activated their workers. It was tricky work getting them all outside the collapsium-walled power-plant area; each worker had to be passed through by the supervisor inside, under Matsui's control. Because of the close quarters at which they worked inside the reactor and the converter, they weren't fitted with anticollision repulsors, and, working under close human supervision, they all had audiovisual pickups. It took some time to get adequate screens set up outside the collapsium.

Finally, they were ready. Their two supervisors went up to the ceiling, one controlled by Conn and the other by Matsui. The larger, egg-shaped shop-labor supervisors were still moving in irregular orbits; those of the workers still able to receive commands were trying to obey them, and the rest were jammed in a swarm at the other end.

First one, and then the other of the labor-boss robots were captured. They were by now at the end of what might, loosely, be called their wits. They weren't used to operating without orders, and had been sending out commands largely at random. Now they came to a stop, and then began moving in tight, guided circles; one by one, the worker robots still able to heed them were brought to ground and turned off. That left the swarm at the door. The worker-robots under direct control of the power-plant supervisors went after them, grappling them and hauling them down to where Anse and Jerry Rivas and Captain Nichols could turn them off manually.

The aircar was a hopeless wreck, but its radio was still functioning. Conn called Charley Gatworth, who called a gang under Gomez, working not far away; they came with another car.

It took all the next day for a gang of six of them to get the place straightened up. Neither Conn nor Gomez, who was a roboticist himself, would trust any of the workers or the two supervisors; their experiences out of control had rendered them unreliable. They took out their power units and left them to be torn down and repaired later. Other robots were brought in to replace them. When they were through, the power-unit cartridge plant was ready for operation.

Jerry Rivas wanted to start production immediately.

"We'll have to go back to Poictesme pretty soon," he said. "We don't want to go back empty. Well, I know that no matter what we dug up, and what we could sell or couldn't sell, there's always a market for power-unit cartridges. Electric-light units, household-appliance units, aircar and airboat units, any size at all. We run that plant at full capacity for a few days and we can load the *Harriet Barne* full, and I'll bet the whole cargo will be sold in a week after we get in."

XV

THE *Harriet Barne* settled comfortably at the dock, the bunting-swathed tugs lifting away from her. They had the outside sound pickups turned as low as possible, and still the noise was deafening. The spaceport was jammed, people on the ground and contragravity vehicles swarming above, with police cars vainly trying to keep them in order. All the bands in Storisende seemed to have been combined; they were blaring the "Planetary Hymn";

> *Genji Gartner's body lies a-moldering in the tomb,*
> *But his soul goes marching on!*

When they opened the airlock, there was a hastily improvised ceremonial barge, actually a farm-scow completely draped in red and white, the Planetary colors. They all stopped, briefly, as they came out, to enjoy the novelty of outdoor air which could actually be breathed. Conn saw his father in the scow, and beside him Sylvie Jacquemont, trying, almost successfully, to keep from jumping up and down in excitement. Morgan Gatworth to meet his son, and Lester Dawes to meet his. Kurt Fawzi, Dolf Kellton, Colonel Zareff, Tom Brangwyn. He didn't see his mother, or his sister. Flora he had hardly counted on, but he was disappointed that his mother wasn't there to meet him.

Sylvie was embracing her father as he shook hands with his; then she threw her arms around his neck.

"Oh, Conn, I'm so happy! I was watching everything I could on-screen, everything you saw, and all the places you were, and everything you were doing. . . ."

The scow—pardon, ceremonial barge—gave a slight lurch,

throwing them together. Over her shoulder, he saw his father and Yves Jacquemont exchanging grins. Then they had to break it up while he shook hands with Fawzi and Judge Ledue and the others, and by the time that was over, the barge was letting down in front of the stand at the end of the dock, and the band was still deafening Heaven with "Genji Gartner's Body," and they all started up the stairs to be greeted by Planetary President Vyckhoven; he looked like an elderly bear who has been too well fed for too long in a zoo. And by Minister-General Murchison, who represented the Terran Federation on Poictesme. He was thin and balding, and he looked as though he had just mistaken the vinegar cruet for the wine decanter. Genji Gartner's soul stopped marching on, but the speeches started, and that was worse. And after the speeches, there was the parade, everybody riding in transparent-bodied air-cars, and the *Lester Dawes* and the two ships of the new Planetary Air Navy and a swarm of gunboats in column five hundred feet above, all firing salutes.

In spite of what wasn't, but might just as well have been, a concerted conspiracy to keep them apart, he managed to get a few words privately with Sylvie.

"My mother; she didn't get here. Is anything wrong?"

"Is anything anything else? I've been in the middle of it ever since you went away. Your mother's still moaning about all these companies your father's promoting—he never used to do anything like that, and it's all too big, and it's going to end in a big smash. And then she gets onto Merlin. You know, she won't say Merlin, she always calls it, 'that thing.' "

"I've noticed that."

"Then she begins talking about all the horrible things that'll happen when it's found, and that sets Flora off. Flora says Merlin's a big fake, and you and your father are using it to rob thousands of widows and orphans of their life savings, and that sets your mother off again. Self-sustaining cyclic reaction, like the Bethe solar-phoenix. And every time I try to pour a little oil on the troubled waters, I find I've gotten it on the fire instead. And then, Flora had this fight with Wade Lucas, and of course, she blames you for that."

127

"Good heavens, why?"

"Well, she couldn't blame it on herself, could she? Oh, you mean why the fight? Lucas is in business with your father now, and she can't convince him that you and your father are a pair of quadruple-dyed villains, I suppose. Anyhow, the engagement is *phttt!* Conn, is my father going back to Koshchei?"

"As soon as we can round up some people to help us on the ship."

"Then I'm going along. I've had it, Conn. I'm a combat-fatigue case."

"But, Sylvie; that isn't any place for a girl."

"Oh, pool! This is Sylvie. We're old war buddies. We soldiered together on Barathrum; remember?"

"Well, you'd be the only girl, and . . ."

"That's what you think. If you expect to get any kind of a gang together, at least a third of them will be girls. A lot of technicians are girls, and when work gets slack, they're always the first ones to get shoved out of jobs. I'll bet there are a thousand girl technicians out of work here—any line of work you want to name. I know what I'll do; I'll make a telecast appearance. I still have some news value, from the Barathrum business. Want to bet that I won't be the working girl's Joan of Arc by this time next week?"

That cheered him. A girl can punch any kind of a button a man can, and a lot of them knew what buttons to punch, and why. Say she could find fifty girls . . .

He had a slightly better chance to talk to his father before the banquet at the Executive Palace that evening. They shared the same suite at the Ritz-Gartner, and even welcoming committees seldom chase their victims from bedroom to bath.

"Yes, I know all about it," Rodney Maxwell said bitterly. "I was home, a couple of weeks ago. Flora simply will not speak to me, and your mother begged me, in tears, to quit everything we're doing here. I tried to give her some idea of what would happen if I dropped this, even supposing I could; she wouldn't listen to me." He finished putting the

THE COSMIC COMPUTER

studs in his shirt. "You still think this is worth what it's costing us?"

"You saw the views we sent back. There's work on Koshchei for a million people, at least. Why, even these two makeshift ships they're putting together here at Storisende are giving work, one way or another, to almost a thousand. Think what things will be like a year from now, if this keeps on."

Rodney Maxwell gave a wry laugh. "Didn't know I had a real Simon-pure altruist for a son."

"Pardner, when you call me that, smile."

"I am smiling. With some slight difficulty."

He didn't think well of the banquet. Back in Litchfield, Senta would have fired half her human help and taken a sledgehammer to her robo-chef for a meal like that. Even his father's camp cook would have been ashamed of it. And there were more speeches.

President Vyckhoven managed to get hold of him and Yves Jacquemont afterward, and steered them into his private study.

"Have you any real reason for thinking that Merlin might be on Koshchei?" the Planetary President asked.

"Great Ghu, no! We weren't looking for Merlin, Mr. President. We were looking for a hypership. We have one, too. Calling her *Ouroboros II.* Twenty-five-hundred-footer. We expect to have her to space in a few months. I surely don't need to tell you what that will do toward restoring planetary prosperity."

"No, of course not; a hypership of our own. But . . ." He looked from one to the other of them. "But I understood . . . That is, Mr. Kurt Fawzi was saying . . ."

"Mr. Fawzi is looking for Merlin here on Poictesme. If anybody finds it, that's where it'll be found. I'm interested in getting business started again. If Merlin is found, it would help, of course." He shrugged.

"Don't look at me," Jacquemont said. "Mr. Maxwell—both of them, father and son—want some spaceships. They hired me to help build them. That's all I have in it." Then he relit the cigar the President had given him and leaned back in his chair, staring at the stuffed alcesoid head with the seven-foot hornspread above the fireplace.

Conn described the interview to his father after they were back at the hotel.

"I hope you convinced him. You know, he's afraid of Merlin. A lot of people have been saying that if Merlin's found, it should be used to determine Government policy. A few extremists are beginning to say that Merlin ought to *be* the Government, and Jake Vyckhoven and his cronies ought to be dumped. Into the handiest mass-energy converter, preferably. You know, if anybody found Merlin and started it auditing the Planetary Treasury, Jake Vyckhoven'd be the one who'd be wanting a hypership."

Tom Brangwyn ran him down the next morning in the dining room.

"Conn, I wish you'd come along with me," he said. "Some of us are up in Kurt's suite; we'd all like to talk to you."

Somehow, he was acting as though he were making an arrest. That might have been nothing but professional habit. Conn went up to Fawzi's suite, and found Fawzi and Judge Ledue and Dolf Kellton and close to a dozen others there.

"I'm glad you could come, Conn," the Judge greeted him. Now that the defendant had arrived, the trial could begin. "I wish your father could have gotten here. I asked him to come, but he had a prior engagement. A meeting with some of the financial people here, about some company he's interested in."

"That's right; Trisystem & Interstellar Spacelines."

"Interstellar!" Kurt Fawzi almost howled. "Great Ghu! Now it isn't enough to go out to Koshchei; he wants to go clear out of the Trisystem. That's what we wanted to talk about; all this nonsense you and your father are in. Merlin's right here on Poictesme. It's right at Force Command, and if your father hadn't robbed us of all our best men, like Jerry Rivas and Anse Dawes, we'd have found it by now. I don't think you and your father care a hoot if we ever find Merlin or not!"

"Kurt, that's a dreadful thing to say," Dolf Kellton objected in a shocked voice.

"It's a dreadful thing to have to say," Fawzi replied, "but you tell me what Conn Maxwell or Rodney Maxwell are doing to help find it."

"Who showed you where Force Command was?" Klem Zareff asked.

Nobody could think of any good quick comeback to that.

Conn took advantage of the pause to ask, "Why do you want to find Merlin?"

"Why do we . . ." Fawzi spluttered indignantly. "If you don't know . . ."

"I know why I do. I want to see if you do. Do you?"

"Merlin would answer so many questions," Dolf Kellton told him gently. "Questions I can't answer for myself."

"With Merlin, we could set up a legal code and a system of jurisprudence that would give everybody absolute justice," Judge Ledue said.

As if absolute justice wasn't the last thing anybody in his right senses would want; a robot-judge would have the whole planet in jail inside a month.

"We have a man who joined us after you went off to Koshchei, Conn," Franz Veltrin said. "A Mr. Carl Leibert. He's some kind of a clergyman, from over Morven way. He says that Merlin could formulate an entirely new religion, which would regenerate humanity."

"Well, I don't have any such lofty ideas," Fawzi said. "I just want Merlin to show us how to get some prosperity here; bring things back to what they were before Poictesme went broke."

"And that's what Father and I are trying to do. You're going into the woods with a book on how to chop down a tree, and no ax." Fawzi looked at him in surprise, started to say something, and thought better of it. "If we want prosperity, we need tools. Our problem is loss of markets. If we find Merlin, and tape it with everything that's happened in the forty years since it was shut down, Merlin will tell us where to find new markets. But the markets won't come to us. We'll have to do our own exporting, and we'll need ships. Now, you men have been studying about Merlin, and hunting for Merlin, all your lives. I can't add anything to what you know, and neither can my father. You find Merlin, and we'll have the ships ready when you do find it."

"Kurt, I think he has a point," somebody said.

"You're blasted well right he has," Klem Zareff put in. "If it wasn't for Conn Maxwell, you know where we'd be? Back in Litchfield, sitting around in Kurt's office, talking about how wonderful things'll be when we find Merlin, and doing nothing to find it."

"Kurt, I believe Conn is entitled to an apology," Judge Ledue ruled. "How close we are to finding Merlin I don't know, but it is due to him that we have any hope of finding it at all."

"Conn, I'm sorry," Fawzi said. "I oughtn't to have said some of the things I did. But we're all on edge; we've been having so much trouble . . . Conn, it's right there at Force Command; I know it is. We've been all over the place. We have shafts sunk at each of the corners; we've used scanners, and put off echo shots. Nothing. We looked for additional passages out of the headquarters; there aren't any. But it has to be somewhere around. It just *has* to be!"

"Maybe if I go out to Force Command with you, I might see something you've overlooked. And if I can't, I'll try to scrape up some stuff on Koshchei for you. Deep-vein scanners, that sort of thing, from the mines."

They took the *Lester Dawes* out at a little past noon and turned south and east. Everybody aboard was happy—except Conn Maxwell. He was thinking of the years and years ahead of these trusting, hopeful old men, each year the grave of another expectation. Two hundred miles from Force Command, the *Goblin* met them, her sides still spalled and dented from the hits she had taken in Barathrum Spaceport. When they came in sight of it, the mesa-top was deserted. Fawzi began wondering where in Nifflheim all the drilling rigs, and the seismo-trucks, were. Somebody with a pair of binoculars called attention to activity on the side of the high butte on top of which the relay station was located. Fawzi began swearing exasperatedly.

"Might be something Mr. Leibert thought of," Franz Veltrin suggested.

"Then why in blazes didn't he screen us about it?"

"Who is this Leibert?" Conn asked. "Somebody mentioned him this morning, I think."

"He joined us after you left, Conn," Dolf Kellton said. "He's a clergyman from Morven. No regular denomination; he has a sect of his own."

"Yah, he would!" Klem Zareff rumbled. "Pious fraud!"

"He's really a good man, Conn; Klem's prejudiced. He says we ought to use Merlin to show us the true nature of God, and how to live in accordance with the Divine Will. He says Merlin can teach us a new religion."

A new religion, based on Merlin; that would be good. And then the fanatics who thought Merlin was the Devil would start a holy war to wipe out the servants of Satan, and with all the combat equipment that was lying around on this planet . . . For the first time since this business started, he began to feel really frightened.

An aircar came bulleting away from the butte and landed on the mesa as the *Lester Dawes* set down. The man who met them at the head of the vertical shaft wore Federation fatigues—baggy trousers, ankle boots and long smock, dyed black. He was bareheaded, and his white hair was almost shoulder-long. He had a white beard.

"Welcome, Brothers," he greeted, a hand raised in benediction. "And who is this with you?"

His voice was high and quavery; not a good pulpit voice, Conn thought.

Kurt Fawzi introduced Conn, and Leibert grasped his hand with a grip that was considerably stronger than his voice.

"Bless you, young man! It is to you alone that we owe our thanks that we are about to find the Great Computer. Every sapient being in the Galaxy will honor your name for a thousand years."

"Well, I hadn't counted on quite that much, Mr. Leibert.

If it'll only help a few of these people to make a decent living I'll be satisfied."

Leibert shook his head sadly. "You think entirely in material terms, young man," he reproved. "Forget these things; acquire the higher spiritual values. The Great Computer must not be degraded to such uses; we should let it show us how to lift ourselves to a high spiritual plane. . . ."

It went on like that, after they went down to Foxx Travis's —now Fawzi's—office, where there were silver-stoppered decanters instead of the old green-glass pitcher, and gold-plated ashtrays, and thick carpets on the floor. The man was a lunatic; he made Fawzi's office gang look frigidly sane. Furthermore, he was an ignoramus. He had no idea what a computer could or couldn't do. Anybody who could build a computer of the sort he thought Merlin was wouldn't need it, he *would* be God.

As he talked, Conn began to be nagged by an odd sense of recognition. He'd seen this Carl Leibert before, somewhere, and somehow he was sure that the long white hair and the untrimmed beard weren't part of the picture. That puzzled him. He doubted if he'd have remembered Leibert from six years ago, almost seven, now, though a lot of itinerant evangelists showed up in Litchfield. That might have been it.

"I tell you, the Great Computer is there, in the heart of the butte," Leibert was insisting, now. "It has been revealed to me in a dream. It is completely buried. After it was made, no human touched it. The men who were here and used it in the War communicated with it only by radio."

That could be so. There were fully robotic computers, intended for use in places where no human could go and live. There was a big one on Nifflheim, armored against the fluorine atmosphere and the hydrofluoric-acid rains. But there was no point in that here, the things were enormously complicated, and military engineering of any sort emphasized simplicity—*Aaaagh!* Was he beginning to believe this balderdash himself?

Klem Zareff fell in with him as they were going to dinner. "Revealed in a dream!" the old Rebel snorted. "One thing

134

you can always get away with lying about is what you dream."

"You think he's lying? I think he's just crazy."

"That's what he wants you to think. Look, Conn, he knows Merlin is here; he's trying to keep us from it. That's why he shifted all that equipment over on the butte. He's working for Sam Murchison."

"I thought your theory was that the Federation had lost Merlin."

"It was, at first. It doesn't look that way to me now. It's right here at Force Command, somewhere. They don't want it found, and they're going to do everything they can to stop us. I oughtn't to have left this fellow Leibert here alone; well, I won't do that again. Get Tom Brangwyn to help me."

XVI

THE VOYAGE back to Koshchei had been a week-long nightmare. When she had been the pride and budget-wrecker of Transcontinent & Overseas Airline, the *Harriet Barne* had accommodated two hundred first-class and five hundred lower-deck passengers, but the conversion to a spaceship had drastically reduced her capacity. The three hundred men and women who had been recruited for the Koshchei colony had been crammed into her with brutal disregard for comfort, privacy or anything else except the ability of the air-recyclers to keep them breathing. When Captain Nichols set her down at the administration building at Port Carpenter, a few had had to be carried off, but they were all alive, which made the trip an unqualified success.

The dozen leaders of the expedition were congratulating themselves on that in one of the executive offices after the first dinner at Port Carpenter. Rodney Maxwell, in Storisende, had joined them in screen-image; he was mostly listening, and sometimes contributing a remark apropos of something the rest of them had said five minutes ago.

"Our hypership," Conn was saying, "is going to have to be item two on the agenda. The first thing we need is a ship for the Poictesme-Koshchei run. By this time next year, we ought to have a thousand to fifteen hundred people here at the least. We can't haul them all on that flying sardine can."

"We'll need supplies, too. What was left here won't last forever," Nichols added.

"And you're going to have to run this at a profit," Luther Chen-Wong, who had come along for first hand experience and to help with adminstrative work, added. "You have a big payroll to meet, and you'll have to keep the stockholders happy. People like Jethro Sastraman and some of these Storisende bankers aren't going to be satisfied with promises and long-term prospects; they'll want dividends."

"We'll have to get claims staked on something besides Port Carpenter, too. Those ships that are building at Storisende will be finished before long," Jerry Rivas said. "If we don't get some more things claimed, the first thing you know, we'll own Port Carpenter and nothing else."

"Well, let's see what we can find in the way of a big airboat, or a small ship," Conn said. "Jerry, you can pick a party for exploring. Just zigzag around the planet and transmit in locations and views of whatever you find, and we'll sent it on to Storisende."

"And don't pick anybody for your exploring party that can't be spared from anything here," Jacquemont added. "We don't want to have to chase you halfway around the world to bring back the only specialist in something yesterday at the latest."

"Are you going to come along, Conn?" Rivas asked.

"Oh, Lord, no! I'm going to be doing fifteen things at once here."

All the computer work. Finding materials to make astrogational equipment and robo-pilots. Studying hyperspace theory—fortunately, there was an excellent library here—and setting up classes, and teaching school. And keeping in touch with his father, on Poictesme. It was making him nervous not to know what sort of foolishness the older and wiser heads might be getting into.

The next morning, they began organizing work-gangs and setting up committees. Three men, two girls and about twenty robots got an open-pit iron mine started; as soon as the steel mill was ready, ore started coming in. Anse Dawes had a gang looking for something they could build a 350-foot interplanetary ship out of; Jacquemont and Mack Vibart were getting plans and specifications and making lists of needed materials. Conn gathered a dozen men and women and started classes in computer theory and practice; at the same time, he and Charley Gatworth were teaching themselves and each other hyperspatial astrogation, which was the art of tossing a ship into some everythingless no-place outside normal space-time, and then pulling her out again by her bootstraps at some other place in the normal continuum, light-years away.

Roughly, it compared to shooting hummingbirds on the wing, blindfolded, with a not particularly accurate pistol, from a mile-a-minute merry-go-round.

That was something you could only do with a computer. A human, with a slide rule, a pencil and pad, could figure it out, of course—if he had fifty-odd thousand years to do it. A good computer did it in thirty seconds. That was one difference between people and computers. The other difference was that the desirability of making a hyperspace jump would never occur to a computer, unless somebody pushed a button and taped in instructions.

They found a three-hundred-foot globular skeleton, probably the nucleus of a big hyperspace ship, and decided that was big enough for what they wanted. The entire colony got to work on it. Photoprinted plans and specifications poured out as Jacquemont and a couple of draftsmen got them up. Steel came out of the steel mill at one end while ore came in at the other. A swarm of big contragravity machines, some robotic and some human-operated, clustered around the skeletal hull like hornets building a nest.

THE COSMIC COMPUTER

Trisystem & Interstellar Spacelines was chartered; the lawyers reported having to overcome a little more resistance than usual from the Government about that. And the bill to nationalize Merlin, which had died in committee, was resuscitated and was being debated hotly on the floor of Parliament. The Administration was now supporting it.

"Are they completely crazy?" Conn wanted to know, when he heard about that. "They pass that bill and nobody's going to look for Merlin if they know the Government will snatch it as soon as they find it."

"That is precisely Jake Vyckhoven's idea," his father replied. "I told you he was afraid of Merlin. He's getting more afraid of it every day."

He had reason to. There was a growing sentiment in favor of turning the entire Government over to the computer as soon as it was found. To his horror, Conn heard himself named as chairman of a committee that should be set up to operate it. The moderates, who had merely wanted Merlin used in an advisory capacity, were dropping out; the agitation was coming from extremists who wanted Merlin to be the whole Government, and now the extremists were developing an extreme wing of their own, who called themselves Cybernarchists and started wearing colored-shirt uniforms and greeting each other with an archaic stiff-arm salute, and the words, "Hail Merlin!"

And the followers of the gospel-shouter on the west coast were now cropping up all over the mainland, and on the continent of Acaire to the north, and another cult, non-religious, was convinced that Merlin was a living machine, with conscious intelligence of its own and awesome psi-powers, a sort of super-Golem, which, if found and awakened, would enslave the whole Galaxy. Fortunately, these two hated each other as venomously as both did the Cybernarchists, and spent most of their energies attacking each other's meetings. The news-services were beginning to publish casualty lists, some heavy enough for outpost fighting between a couple of regular armies.

One thing, it helped the employment situation. Everybody was hiring mercenaries.

138

"But what," Conn asked, "are the sane people doing?"

"You ought to know," his father told him. "I suspect that you have all of them on Koshchei now."

The sane people, if that was what they were, were being busy. They were putting a set of Abbott lift-and-drive engines together, and Conn's computer class was estimating the mass of the finished ship and the amount of energy needed to overcome gravitation and give it constant acceleration from Koshchei to Poictesme. They were learning, by trial and error, largely error, how to build a set of pseudograv engines. And they were putting together a hundred and one other things, all of which was good training for the time they'd be ready to start work on *Ouroboros II*.

Jerry Rivas had found a contragravity craft which seemed to have been used by some top official for business and inspection trips, had gathered a crew of non-specialists who weren't urgently needed at Port Carpenter, and set out to circumnavigate the planet. It worked just the reverse of expectation. He found a big uranium mine, with an isotope-separation plant and a battery of plutonium-breeders; that meant that Mohammed Matsui and half a dozen other nuclear-power people had to get into another boat and speed after him to see what he had really found. As soon as they landed, Rivas took off again to discover a copper mine and a complex of smelters and processing plants. That took a few more experts, or reasonable facsimiles, away from Port Carpenter. And then he found a whole city that manufactured nothing but computers and robo-controls and things like that.

Conn loaded his whole computer-theory class onto a freight-scow and took them there. By the time he landed, his father was screening him from Storisende.

"When are you going to get the ship finished?" he was asking. "Kurt Fawzi's pestering the daylights out of me. He wants that equipment you promised him."

"We're working on it. What's happened, has Carl Leibert had another revelation?"

"I don't know about that. Kurt's sure Merlin is directly

under Force Command. And speaking about Leibert, Klem Zareff's been after me about him. You know I've contracted for the full-time and exclusive services of this Barton-Massarra detective agency. Well, Klem wants me to put them to work investigating Leibert."

"Yes, I know; Leibert's a Terran Federation spy. Why do you need the full-time services of the biggest private detective agency on Poictesme?"

"There have been some odd things happening. People have been trying to bribe and intimidate some of my office help. I have found microphones and screen-pickups planted around. I caught one of our clerks trying to make copies of voice-tapes. I think it's some of these other Merlin-chasing companies, trying to find out how close we are to it. Klem Zareff is recruiting more guards. But how soon are you going to get that ship built?"

"We're working on it. That's all I know, now."

He went back to work getting a classroom ready for his students. If he'd accepted that instructorship at Montevideo, he wouldn't be a full professor now, but none of the rest of this would be happening, either.

That night, he had the dream about starting the big machine and not being able to stop it again.

There was street-fighting in Storisende between the Cybernarchists and Government troops. There was a pitched battle in the west between the Armageddonists (Merlin-is-Satan) and the Human Supremacy League (Merlin-is-the-Golem), with heavy losses and claims of victory on both sides. President Vyckhoven proclaimed planet-wide martial law, and then discovered that he had nothing to enforce it with.

Luther Chen-Wong screened him from Port Carpenter. His voice was almost inaudibly low at first.

"Conn, I just had a call from Jerry and Clyde. I think we can knock off work on that ship we're building now. We won't need it."

"Have they found a ship?" If they had, it would be the first one anybody had found. "Where?"

"They haven't found *a* ship, Conn; they've found all of them. All the ships in the Alpha System except the *Harriet Barne* and the two they're building at Storisende. The place is marked on the map as Sickle Mountain Naval Observatory. It's just a bitty little dot, but the map was made before the evacuation started. It's where most of the troops in the system were embarked on hyperships, I think. Wait till I show you the views."

Conn put on another screen; the first view was from an altitude of five miles. He didn't need Luther's voice to identify Sickle Mountain; a long curve, with a spur at right angles to one end, the name must have suggested itself to whoever saw it first. The observatory had been built where the handle of the sickle joined the blade; as the ship from which the view had been taken had approached, the details grew plainer. At the same time, it became evident that the plain inside the curve of the sickle was powdered with tiny sparkles, like tinsel dust on red-brown velvet.

"Great Ghu, are those all ships?"

"That's right. Look at this one, now."

The view changed. The aircraft was down, now, below the crest of the mountain, circling slowly above the plain. Hundreds, no, over a thousand, of them; two- and three- and five-hundred-footers, and here and there a thousand-footer that could have been converted into a hypership if anybody had wanted to take the trouble. The view changed again; this time from an aircar dropped from the ship, he supposed; it was down almost to the tops of the ships, and he could read names and home ports: *Pixie*, Chloris; *Helen O'Loy*, Anaïtis. They were from Jurgen. *Sky-Rover*, Port Saunders; she was from Horvendile. Ships from Storisende, and Yellowmarsh on Janicot, and . . .

"Now we know where they all went."

It was logical, of course. Most of the hyperships used in the evacuation had been built here. It had been less trouble to lead the troops and the civilian workers from Poictesme and the other planets onto small normal-space ships and bring them here than to take the big ships away on short interplanetary runs to the other planets.

"Have you screened my father yet?"

"Yes. This is going to knock the bottom out of the companies that are building those ships at Storisende, I'm afraid."

"Their tough luck."

"It could be everybody's tough luck. Both those companies have been issuing stock, and there's been a lot of speculation in it. This market's so inflated now that a puncture at one place might blow the whole thing out."

He knew that. He shrugged. "Father will have to think of something. Tell him I'll screen him from Sickle Mountain."

Then he went back to his classroom.

"All right, class dismissed," he said. "You have twenty minutes to get your bags packed. We're going to work for real, now."

Airboats and airships flocked to Sickle Mountain; some of them hastened back to Port Carpenter for loads of food, for there was none in the storehouses at the embarkation camp. They inspected ship after ship, and chose two three-hundred-footers. They sent airships and freight-scows to the dozen-odd cities and industrial centers that had been already explored, to gather cargo, as far as possible the items in shortest supply on Poictesme.

"Don't worry about a market smash," his father told him. "We have that taken care of. Trisystem Investments has just bought up a lot of stock in both of those companies, and we've set up agreements with them—informally, of course; we'll have to get them voted on by our own companies— to sell them ships from Koshchei. In return, the company that's building the ship out of four air-freighters will go to Janicot, and the company that's building a ship out of the old Leitzenring Building will go to Jurgen, and they'll both stay off Koshchei. Sterber, Flynn & Chen-Wong will probably be defending antitrust suits till the end of time. The Planetary Government has stopped liking us, you know."

"Then we'll have to get one that will like us. There'll be an election about this time next year, won't there?"

His father nodded. "To use one of your expressions, we're working on it. How soon can you get your ships in?"

"We'll be loaded and ready to lift off in a week. Another week for the trip."

"Well, don't forget that equipment you promised Kurt Fawzi."

"We'll have that on. Jerry Rivas is gathering it up now."

"How are you fixed for arms on Koshchei?"

"Arms? Why, there are some. There was a pretty big force of Space Marines on duty here, and they left everything they couldn't carry in their hands. Why? The Armageddonists and the Cybernarchists and Human Supremacy bought all you had on hand?"

"They're buying, but I wasn't thinking of that. I was thinking that your crews might need something to argue their way off the ships at Storisende with. Things are getting just slightly rugged here, now."

XVII

THERE WERE no bands or speeches when they came in this time. A lot of contragravity vehicles circled widely around the spaceport, but except for a few news-service cars, the police were keeping them back of a two-mile radius around the landing-pits. A couple of gunboats were making tight circles above, and on the dock were more vehicles and a horde of police and guards.

When Rodney Maxwell came across the bridge from the dock after they opened the airlocks, he was followed by a dozen Barton-Massarra private police, as villainous-looking a collection of ruffians as Conn had ever seen. He was wearing a new suit, with a waist-length jacket instead of the long coat he usually wore, and there was a holstered automatic on each hip. In Litchfield, he never carried more than one pistol, and Storisende was supposed to be an orderly place where nobody needed to go armed. More than anything else, that told Conn approximately what had been going on while he had been on Koshchei.

"Ship-guard," his father told Yves Jacquemont. "All your crew can come off; they'll take care of things. Get your people in that troop carrier over there. Everybody will stay at Interplanetary Building. None of the hotels are safe, not even the Ritz-Gartner. And be sure everybody's well armed when they come off the ship."

Jacquemont nodded. "I know the drill; I've been in Port Oberth on Venus and Skorvann on Loki. Any law we want, we make for ourselves."

"That's about it. I'll see you there. Conn, I wish you'd come with me. Somebody here wants to talk to you."

He wondered if his mother, or Flora, had come to Storisende. When he asked his father as they crossed onto the dock, there was a brief twinge of pain in Rodney Maxwell's face.

"No, they're not having anything to do—*Duck; quick!*"

Then his father was diving under a lifter-truck that stood empty on the dock. The private police were scattering for cover, and an auto-cannon began pom-pomming. Conn took one quick look in the direction in which it was firing, saw an aircar that had broken through the police line and was rushing toward them, and dived under the lifter after his father. As he did, he saw a missile flash out from one of the gunboats like a thrown knife. Then he huddled beside his father and put his arms over his head.

He felt the heat and shock of the explosion and, an instant later, heard the roar. When nothing immediately disastrous happened after he had counted fifteen seconds, he stuck his head out and looked up. The gunboat was struggling to regain her equilibrium, and the aircar had vanished in a fireball. They both emerged, straightening. His father was brushing himself with his hands and saying something about always having to duck under something when he had a new suit on.

"Robot control, probably; could have been launched from anywhere in town. Why, no; your mother and Flora aren't

144

speaking to either of us, any more. Pity, of course, but I'm glad they're in Litchfield. It's a little healthier there."

They walked to the slim recon-car and climbed in, pulling the door shut after them. Wade Lucas was waiting for them at the controls.

"There, you see!" he began, as soon as he had the car lifting. "What I've been telling you. We'll have to stop this."

"Conn, meet our new partner. I told him everything you told me, out on the Mall, the day you came home. I had to," his father hastened to add. "He'd figured most of it out for himself. The only thing to do was admit him to the lodge and give him the oath."

"I didn't know about General Travis; I didn't even know he was still alive," Lucas said. "But the rest of it was pretty obvious, once I stopped jumping to conclusions and did a little thinking. You know, ever since I came here I've been preaching to these people to stop looking for Merlin and do something to help themselves. You're smarter than I am, Conn; instead of opposing them, you're guiding them."

"Did you tell Flora?"

Lucas shook his head. "I tried to explain what you're trying to do, but she wouldn't listen. She just told me I'd gotten to be as big a crook as you two." He had the car up to fifty thousand; putting it into a wide circle around the city, he locked the controls and got out his cigarettes. "Rod, we've got to stop this. You were just lucky this time. Some of these days your luck's going to run out."

"How can we stop?" Conn demanded. "Tell them the truth? They'd lynch us, and then go on hunting for Merlin."

"Worse than that; it'd be a smash worse than the one when the War ended. I was only ten then, but I can remember that very plainly. We can't stop it, and we wouldn't dare stop it if we could."

"What's been going on here in the last month?" Conn asked. "I've been too busy to keep in touch. I know there's been rioting, and these crackpot sects, but . . ."

"I think this is personal to us. There have been some ugly things happening. There were four attempts to burglarize our offices. I told you about some of the other stuff, the microphones we found, and so on. The worst thing was Lucy Nocero, my secretary. She just vanished, a couple of weeks ago. Three days later, the police found her wandering in a park, a complete imbecile. Somebody who either didn't know how to use one or didn't care what happened had used a mind-probe on her. It's twenty to one she'll never recover."

"It's this Storisende financial crowd," Wade Lucas said. "They had things all their own way till Alpha-Interplanetary was organized. Now they're getting shoved into the background, and they don't like it."

"They're making more money than they ever did, and they just love it," Rodney Maxwell said. "I'd think it was either Jake Vyckhoven or Sam Murchison."

"Murchison!" Lucas hooted. "Why, he's nobody! Federation Minister-General; all the authority of the Terran Federation, and nothing to enforce it with. He doesn't have a position, here; he has a disease. Sleeping sickness."

"He certainly doesn't believe there is a Merlin, does he?" Conn asked.

"I don't know what he believes, but he's getting to be Klem Zareff's opposite number. He thinks this whole thing's a plot against the Federation. It's a good thing Klem didn't get around to repainting his combat vehicles black and green, the way he did the Home Guard stuff at Litchfield."

"I'd be more likely to think it was Vyckhoven."

"Could be. Or it could be the Armageddonists, or Human Supremacy; I am ashamed to say that this heil-Merlin Cybernarchist gang are friendly to us. Or it could be some of the banking crowd, or some of these rival space-companies. Barton-Massarra is trying to find out. Well, we have some of Wade's pet suspects at Interplanetary Building now. There's been a meeting going for the last week to partition the Alpha Gartner System."

The Interplanetary Building had been a medium-class residence hotel at the time of the War. Junior staff officers and civilian technicians and their families had lived there. It had been vacant ever since the disastrous outbreak of peace. Now it had a big new fluorolite sign, and housed the

THE COSMIC COMPUTER

offices of all the Maxwell companies. There was a truculent display of anti-vehicle weapons on the top landing stage, and more Barton-Massarra private police. They looked even more villainous then the ones at the spaceport. Conn recalled having heard that most of the Blackie Perales gang had been discharged for lack of evidence; he wondered how many of them had hired with Barton-Massarra.

The meeting was in a big conference room six floors down; it had been going on uninterrupted for days, with all the interested companies' representatives standing watch-and-watch around the clock. Lester Dawes and Morgan Gatworth and Lorenzo Menardes were there for L E. & S.; Transcontinent & Overseas was represented; there were people from Alpha-Interplanetary, and bankers and financiers, and people from the companies building the two ships at the spaceport. And J. Fitzwilliam Sterber, the lawyer.

And reporters, phoning stories in and getting audiovisual interviews of anybody who would hold still long enough. They converged in a rush as Conn and his father and Lucas came in.

"No statement, gentlemen!" Rodney Maxwell shouted, above the babble of their questions. "When we have anything to release, it will be released to all of you."

Jacquemont and Nichols had already arrived; Lucas went to them and began talking about stevedores and lifters to get off the cargoes from the ships. Conn hastened to join them.

"The scanning and mining equipment aboard the *Helen O'Loy*," he said. "That shouldn't be unloaded here; we'll take the ship out to Force Command and unload it there."

Out of the corner of his eye, he saw a lurking reporter snatch the handphone off his radio and begin talking; it would be stated authoritatively that Merlin was at Force Command and would be uncovered as soon as special equipment from Koshchei arrived.

Everybody at the long table was shouting at everybody else. The Jurgen and Janicot Companies wanted to buy ships from Koshchei Exploitation & Development. The Alpha-Interplanetary director, who was also a vice-president

147

of Transcontinent & Overseas, opposed that; another director of A-I, who was also board chairman of Koshchei Exploitation & Development, wanted to sell ships to anybody who had the price, the Transcontinent & Overseas man was calling him a traitor to the company, and one of the stockbrokers, who was also a vice-president of Trisystem Investments and a director of Trisystem & Interstellar Spacelines, was wanting to know which company. And a banker who was stockholder in all the companies was shouting that they were all a gang of crooks, and J. Fitzwilliam Sterber was declaring that anybody who called him a crook could continue the discussion through seconds.

Conn suddenly realized that dueling had never been illegal on Poictesme. He wondered how many duels this meeting was going to hatch.

The next afternoon the *Helen O'Loy* was unloaded, all but the mining equipment; Conn and Yves Jacquemont and Charley Gatworth and a few others took her out to Force Command. They were met by Klem Zareff's armed airboats two hundred and fifty miles from the mesa, and they found the place in more of a state of siege than when the Badlands had been full of outlaws. A lot of heavy armament seemed to have been moved in from Barathrum Spaceport, and Zareff had more men and firepower than he had ever commanded during the System States War. If Minister-General Murchison was convinced that the Merlin excitement was a cover for some seditious plot against the Federation, this ought to give him food for thought.

There was still work, mostly boring lateral shafts for echo shots, going on at the butte, under the relay station. That was Leibert, who was still insisting that that was where Merlin was buried. There was also some work on top of the mesa, by those who were convinced that that was where Merlin was to be found. Kurt Fawzi was taking the lead in that. Franz Veltrin and Dolf Kellton sided with Leibert, and Fawzi's office clique had split into two factions. Judge Ledue was maintaining strict impartiality, as befitted his judicial position.

"Why hasn't your father gotten those detectives of his to work on this fake preacher?" Zareff wanted to know, when he and Tom Brangwyn were able to talk to Conn alone.

"Well, they've been busy," Conn said. "Trying to keep him alive, for one thing. You heard about the robo-bomb somebody launched at us the day we brought the ships in, didn't you?"

"Yes, and we heard about the Nocero girl, too," Brangwyn said. "But hasn't it ever occurred to you or your dad that this fellow that calls himself Leibert might be mixed up with the gang that did that?"

"You suspect him, too?"

Brangwyn nodded. "I took a few audiovisuals of him, when he didn't know it; I sent them to some different law-enforcement people over in Morven, where he says he comes from. They never saw him before, and couldn't find anybody who did."

"Well? He just doesn't have a police record, then."

"He says he's a preacher. Preachers don't go off in the woods by themselves to preach; they get up in pulpits, in front of a lot of people. Those towns over in Morven are small enough for everybody to have known something about him. He's a fake, I tell you."

"Let me have copies of those audiovisuals, Tom. I'll see what can be found out about him. I'm beginning to wonder about him myself. I'm sure I've seen him, somewhere . . ."

When he got back to Storisende, he found that the marathon conference on the sixth floor down at the Interplanetary Building had finally come to an end. Everybody seemed satisfied, and apparently nobody was going to have pistols and coffee with anybody else about it.

"We have things fixed up," his father told him. "The gang who are building the ship out of four air-freighters are chartered as Janicot Industries, Ltd.; they're going to specialize in chemical products. The other company has a charter now, too. They're going to operate on Jurgen and Horvendile. We'll sell them ships, and Alpha-Interplanetary will put on scheduled trips to all three planets and also Koshchei. We're getting along very nicely with them, except that everybody's competing for technicians and skilled labor. We have two hundred more people signed up for Koshchei. What you want to do is train as many of them as you can for ship-operation. Alpha-Interplanetary is going to start a training program here at Storisende; you'd better leave one of your ships for them to work on, and send back as many ships as you can find officers and crews for."

"We're getting things really started."

"Yes. The only trouble is . . ." His father frowned. "I don't understand these people, Conn. Everybody ought to be making millions out of this by this time next year, but all any of them, even these Storisende bankers, can talk about is how soon we're going to find Merlin."

"I wish we could stop that, somehow. Listen; I have it. Merlin never was on Poictesme; Merlin was a space-station a few thousand miles off-planet; there was a crew of operators aboard, and they communicated with Force Command by radio. When the War ended, they took it outside the system and shot off a planetbuster inside her. No more Merlin. How would that be?"

His father shook his head. "Wouldn't do. If anybody believed it, which I doubt, they'd just quit. The market would collapse, everybody would be broke, it would just be the end of the War all over again. Conn, we can't let it stop now. We're going too fast to stop; if we tried it, we'd smash up and break our necks."

XVIII

JERRY RIVAS, Mack Vibart and Luther Chen-Wong had been keeping things running on Koshchei. Work on the interplanetary ship at Port Carpenter had stopped when the Sickle Mountain ships had been found; it had never been resumed. When Conn returned, he found work started on the *Ouroboros II*. Some of the two hundred newcomers who came in on the *Helen O'Loy* had special skills needed on the hypership; most of them went with Clyde Nichols and Charley Gatworth to Sickle Mountain to train as normal-space officers and crewmen. Some of them, it was hoped, would later qualify for hyperspace work. Sylvie, who had been one of the star pupils in the computer class, was now helping him with the long lists of needed materials, some of which had to be brought from other places as much as a thousand miles away. Jerry Rivas went back to exploring; Nichols had to drop his space-training work temporarily to organize a fleet of air-freighters; usually, the men best able to operate them were urgently needed on some job at the construction dock.

Ships lifted out almost daily from Sickle Mountain. They tried to get some kind of salable cargo for each one, without depriving themselves of what they needed for themselves. Some of the ships came back loaded with provisions and bringing new recruits—for instance, the teaching of physics and mathematics almost stopped at Storisende College because the professors had been virtually shanghaied.

Conn found himself losing touch with affairs on Poictesme. Ships had landed on both Janicot and Horvendile and were sending back claims to abandoned factories. By that time they had all the decks into the *Ouroboros II*, and he was working aboard, getting the astrogational and hyperspace instruments put in place. The hypership *Andromeda* was back from the Gamma System; there was close secrecy about what the expedition had found, but the newscasts were full of conjectures about Merlin, and the market went into another dizzy upward spiral. Litchfield Exploration & Salvage opened a huge munitions depot, and combat equipment, once almost unsalable, was selling as fast as it came out. The Government was buying some, but by no means all of it.

"Conn, can you come back here to Poictesme for a while?" his father asked. "Things have turned serious. I don't like to talk about it by screen—too many people know our scrambler combinations. But I wish you were here."

He started to object; there were millions, well, a couple of hundred, things he had to attend to. The look on his father's face stopped him.

"Ship leaving Sickle Mountain tomorrow morning," he said. "I'll be aboard."

The voyage back to Poictesme was a needed rest. He felt refreshed when he got off at Storisende Spaceport and was met by his father and Wade Lucas in one of the slim reconcars. They greeted him briefly and took the car up and away from the city, where it was safe to talk.

"Conn, I'm scared," his father said. "I'm beginning to think there really is a Merlin, after all."

"Oh, come off it! I know it's contagious, but I thought you'd been vaccinated."

"I'm beginning to think so, too," Lucas said. "I don't like it at all."

"You know what that gang who took the *Andromeda* to Panurge found?"

"They were looking for the plant that fabricated the elements for Merlin, weren't they?"

"Yes. They found it. My Barton-Massarra operatives got to some of the crew. This place had been turning out material for a computer of absolutely unconventional design; the two computermen they had with them couldn't make head or tail of half of it. And every blueprint, every diagram, every scrap of writing or recording, had been destroyed. But they found one thing, a big empty fiber folder that had fallen under something and been overlooked. It was marked: TOP SECRET. PROJECT MERLIN."

"Project Merlin could have been anything," Conn started to say. No. Project Merlin was something they made computer parts for.

"Dolf Kellton's research crew, at the Library here, came across some references to Project Merlin, too. For instance, there was a routine division court-martial, a couple of second lieutenants, on a very trivial charge. Force Command ordered the court-martial stopped, and the two officers simply dropped out of the Third Force records, it was stated that they were engaged in work connected with Project Merlin. That's an example; there were half a dozen things like that."

"Tell him what Kurt Fawzi and his crew found," Wade Lucas said.

"Yes. They have a fifty-foot shaft down from the top of the mesa almost to the top of the underground headquarters. They found something on top of the headquarters; a disc-shaped mass, fifty feet thick and a hundred across, armored in collapsium. It's directly over what used to be Foxx Travis's office."

"That's not a tenth big enough for anything that could even resemble Merlin."

"Well, it's something. I was out there day before yesterday. They're down to the collapsium on top of this thing; I rode down the shaft in a jeep and looked at it. Look, Conn, we don't know what this Project Merlin was; all this lore about Merlin that's grown up since the War is pure supposition."

"But Foxx Travis told me, categorically, that there was no Merlin Project," Conn said. "The War's been over forty years; it's not a military secret any longer. Why would he lie to me?"

"Why did you lie to Kurt Fawzi and the others and tell them there was a Merlin? You lied because telling the truth would hurt them. Maybe Travis had the same reason for lying to you. Maybe Merlin's too dangerous for anybody to be allowed to find."

"Great Ghu, are you beginning to think Merlin is the Devil, or Frankenstein's Monster?"

"It might be something just as bad. Maybe worse. I don't think a man like Foxx Travis would lie if he didn't have some overriding moral obligation to."

"And we know who's been making most of the trouble for us, too," Lucas added.

"Yes," Rodney Maxwell said, "we do. And sometime I'm going to invite Klem Zareff to kick my pants-seat. Sam Murchison, the Terran Federation Minister-General."

"How'd you get that?"

"Barton-Massarra got some of it; they have an operative planted in Murchison's office. And some of our banking friends got the rest. This Human Supremacy League is being financed by somebody. Every so often, their treasurer makes a big deposit at one of the banks here, all Federation currency, big denomination notes. When I asked them to, they started keeping a record of the serial numbers and checking withdrawals. The money was paid out, at the First Planetary Bank, to Mr. Samuel S. Murchison, in person. The Armegeddonists are getting money, too, but they're too foxy to put theirs through the banks. I believe they're the ones who mind-probed Lucy Nocero. Barton-Massarra believe, but they can't prove, that Human Supremacy launched that robo-bomb at us, that time at the spaceport."

"Have you done anything with those audiovisuals of Leibert?"

"Gave them to Barton-Massarra. They haven't gotten anything, yet."

"So we have to admit that Klem wasn't crazy after all. What do you want me to do?"

"Go out to Force Command and take charge. We have to assume that there may be a Merlin, we have to assume that it may be dangerous, and we have to assume that Kurt Fawzi and his covey of Merlinolators are just before digging it up. Your job is to see that whatever it is doesn't get loose."

The trouble was, if he started giving orders around Force Command he'd stop being a brilliant young man and become a half-baked kid, and one word from him and the older and wiser heads would do just what they pleased. He wondered if the pro-Leibert and anti-Leibert factions were still squabbling; maybe if he went out of his way to antagonize one side, he'd make allies of the other. He took the precaution of screening in, first; Kurt Fawzi, with whom he talked, was almost incoherent with excitement. At least, he was reasonably sure that none of Klem Zareff's trigger-happy mercenaries would shoot him down coming in.

The well, fifty feet in diameter, went straight down from

the top of the mesa; as the headquarters had been buried under loose rubble, they'd had to vitrify the sides going down. He let down into the hole in a jeep, and stood on the collapsium roof of whatever it was they had found. It wasn't the top of the headquarters itself; the microray scannings showed that. It was a drum-shaped superstructure, a sort of underground penthouse. And there they were stopped. You didn't cut collapsium with a cold chisel, or even an atomic torch. He began to see how he was going to be able to take charge here.

"You haven't found any passage leading into it?" he asked, when they were gathered in Fawzi's—formerly Foxx Travis's—office.

"Nifflheim, no! If we had, we'd be inside now." Tom Brangwyn swore. "And we've been all over the ceiling in here, and we can't find anything but vitrified rock and then the collapsium shielding."

"Sure. There are collapsium-cutters, at Port Carpenter, on Koshchei. They do it with cosmic rays."

"But collapsium will stop cosmic rays," Zareff objected.

"Stop them from penetrating, yes. A collapsium-cutter doesn't penetrate; it abrades. Throws out a rotary beam and works like a grinding-wheel, or a buzz-saw."

"Well, could you get one down that hole?" Judge Ledue asked.

He laughed. "No. The thing is rather too large. In the first place, there's a full-sized power-reactor, and a mass-energy converter. With them, you produce negamatter—atoms with negatively charged protons and positive electrons, positrons. Then, you have to bring them into contact with normal positive-matter— That's done in a chamber the size of a fifty-gallon barrel, made of collapsium and weighing about a hundred tons. Then you have to have a pseudo-grav field to impart rotary motion to your cosmic-ray beam, and the generator door that would lift ten ships the size of the *Lester Dawes*. Then you need another fifty to a hundred tons of collapsium to shield your cutting-head. The cutting-head alone weighs three tons. The rotary beam that does the cutting," he mentioned as an afterthought, "is about the size of a silver five-centisol piece."

Nobody said anything for a few seconds. Carl Leibert stated that Divine Power would aid them. Nobody paid much attention; Leibert's stock seemed to have gone bearish since he had found nothing in the butte and Fawzi had found that whatever-it-was on top of Force Command.

"Means we're going to dig the whole blasted top off, clear down to where that thing is," Zareff said. "That'll take a year."

"Oh, no. Maybe a couple of weeks, after we get started," Conn told them. "It'll take longer to get the stuff loaded on a ship and hauled here than it will to get that thing uncovered and opened."

He told them about the machines they used in the iron mines on Koshchei, and as he talked, he stopped worrying about how he was going to take charge here. He had just been unanimously elected Indispensable Man.

"Bless you, young man!" Carl Leibert cried. "At last, the Great Computer! Those who come after will reckon this the Year Zero of the Age of Regeneration. I will go to my chamber and return thanks in prayer."

"He's been doing a lot of praying lately," Tom Brangwyn remarked, after Leibert had gone out. "He's moved into the chaplain's quarters, back of the pandenominational chapel on the fourth level down. Always keeps his door locked, too."

"Well, if he wants privacy for his devotions, that's his business. Maybe we could all do with a little prayer," Veltrin said.

"Probably praying to Sam Murchison by radio," Klem Zareff retorted. "I'd like to see inside those rooms of his."

He called Yves Jacquemont at Port Carpenter after dinner. When he told Jacquemont what he wanted and why, the engineer remarked that it was a pity screens couldn't be fitted with olfactory sensors, so that he could smell Conn's breath.

"I am not drunk. I am not crazy. And I am not exercising my sense of humor. I don't know what Fawzi and his gang have here, but if it isn't Merlin it's something just as hot.

We want at it, soonest, and we'll have to dig a couple of hundred feet of rock off it and open a collapsium can."

"How are we going to get that stuff on a ship?"

"Anything been done to that normal-space job we started since I saw it last? Can you find engines for it? And is there anything about those mining machines or the cutter that would be damaged by space-radiation or re-entry heat?"

Yves Jacquemont was silent for a good deal longer than the interplanetary time-lag warranted. Finally he nodded.

"I get it, Conn. We won't put the things in a ship; we'll build a ship around them. No; that stuff can all be hauled open to space. They use things like that at space stations and on asteroids and all sorts of places. We'll have to stop work on *Ouroboros,* though."

"Let *Ouroboros* wait. We are going to dig up Merlin, and then everybody is going to be rich and happy, and live happily forever after."

Jacquemont looked at him, silent again for longer than the usual five and a half minutes.

"You almost said that with a straight face." After all, Jacquemont hadn't been cleared yet for the Awful Truth About Merlin, but, like his daughter, he'd been doing some guessing. "I wish I knew how much of this Merlin stuff you believe."

"So do I, Yves. Maybe after we get this thing open, I'll know."

To give himself a margin of safety, Jacquemont had estimated the arrival of the equipment at three weeks. A week later, he was on-screen to report that the skeleton ship— they had christened her *The Thing,* and when Conn saw screen views of her he understood why—was finished and the collapsium-cutter and two big mining machines were aboard. Evidently nobody on Koshchei had done a stroke of work on anything else.

"Sylvie's coming along with her; so are Jerry Rivas and Anse Dawes and Ham Matsui and Gomez and Karanja and four or five others. They'll be ready to go to work as soon as she lands and unloads," Jacquemont added.

That was good; they were all his own people, unconnected with any of the Merlin-hunting factions at Force Command. In case trouble started, he could rely on them.

"Well, dig out some shootin'-irons for them," he advised. "They may need them here."

Depending, of course, on what they found when they opened that collapsium can on top of Force Command, and how the people there reacted to it.

The Thing took a hundred and seventy hours to make the trip; conditions in the small shielded living quarters and control cabin were apparently worse than on the *Harriet Barne* on her second trip to Koschchei. Everybody at Force Command was anxious and excited. Carl Leibert kept to his quarters most of the time, as though he had to pray the ship across space.

At the same time, reports of the near completion of *Ouroboros II* were monopolizing the newscasts, to distract public attention from what was happening at Force Command. Cargo was being collected for her; instead of washing their feet in brandy, next year people would be drinking water. Lorenzo Menardes had emptied his warehouses of everything over a year old; so had most of the other distillers up and down the Gordon Valley. Melon and tobacco planters were talking about breaking new ground and increasing their cultivated acreage for the next year. Agricultural machinery was in demand and bringing high prices. So were stills, and tobacco-factory machinery. It began to look as though the Maxwell Plan was really getting started.

It was decided to send the hypership to Baldur on her first voyage; that was Wade Lucas's suggestion. He was going with her himself, to recruit scientific and technical graduates from his alma mater, the University of Paris-on-Baldur, and from the other schools there. Conn was enthusiastic about that, remembering the so-called engineers on Koschchei, running around with a monkey-wrench in one hand and a textbook in the other, trying to find out what they were supposed to do while they were doing it. Poictesme had been living for too long on the leavings of wartime production; too few people had bothered learning how to produce anything.

The Thing finally settled onto the mesa-top. It looked like something from an old picture of the construction work on one of the Terran space-stations in the First Century. Immediately, every piece of contragravity equipment in the place converged on her; men dangled on safety lines hundreds of feet above the ground, cutting away beams and braces with torches. The two giant mining machines, one after the other, floated free on their own contragravity and settled into place. *The Thing* lifted, still carrying the collapsium-cutting equipment, and came to rest on the brushgrown flat beyond, out of the way.

If Yves Jacquemont had overestimated the time required to get the equipment loaded and lifted off from Koshchei, Conn had been overoptimistic about the speed with which the top of the mesa could be stripped off. Digging away the rubble with which the pit had been filled, and even the solid rock around it, was easier than getting the stuff out of the way. Farm-scows came in from all over, as fast as they and pilots for them could be found; the rush to get brandy and tobacco to Storisende had caused an acute shortage of vehicles.

One by one, the members of the old Fawzi's Office gang came drifting in—Lorenzo Menardes, Morgan Gatworth, Lester Dawes. None of them had any skills to contribute, but they brought plenty of enthusiasm. Rodney Maxwell came whizzing out from Storisende now and then to watch the progress of the work. Of all the crowd, he and Conn watched the two steel giants strip away the tableland with apprehension instead of hope. No, there was a third. Carl Leibert had stopped secluding himself in his quarters; he still talked rapturously about the miracles Merlin would work, but now and then Conn saw him when he thought he was unobserved. His face was the face of a condemned man.

The *Ouroboros II* was finished. The whole planet saw, by screen, the ship lift out; watched from the ship the dwindling away of Koshchei and saw Poictesme grow ahead of her. Twelve hours before she landed, work at Force Command

159

stopped. Everybody was going to Storisende—Sylvie, whose father would command her on her voyage to Baldur, Morgan Gatworth, whose son would be first officer and astrogator, everybody. Except Carl Leibert.

"Then I'm not going either," Klem Zareff decided. "Somebody's got to stay here and keep an eye on that snake."

"No, nor me," Tom Brangwyn said. "And if he starts praying again, I'm going to go and pray along with him."

Conn stayed, too, and so did Jerry Rivas and Anse Dawes. They watched the newscast of the lift-out, a week later. It was peaceful and harmonious; everybody, regardless of their attitudes on Merlin, seemed agreed that this was the beginning of a new prosperity for the planet. There were speeches. The bands played "Genji Gartner's Body," and the "Spaceman's Hymn."

And, at the last, when the officers and crew were going aboard, Conn saw his sister Flora clinging to Wade Lucas's arm. She was one of the small party who went aboard for a final farewell. When she came off, along with Sylvie, she was wiping her eyes, and Sylvie was comforting her. Seeing that made Conn feel better even than watching the ship itself lift away from Storisende.

XIX

WHEN SYLVIE returned from Storisende, she had Flora with her. Conn's sister greeted him embarrassedly; Sylvie led both of them out of the crowd and over to the edge of the excavation.

"Go ahead, Flora," she urged. "Make up with Conn. It won't be any harder than making up with Wade was."

"How did that happen, by the way?" Conn asked.

"Your girlfriend," Flora said. "She came to the house and

practically forced me into a car and flew me into Storisende, and then made me keep quiet and listen while Wade told me the truth."

"I wasn't completely sure what the truth was myself till Wade opened up," Sylvie admitted. "I had a pretty good idea, though."

"I always hated that Merlin thing," Flora burst out. "All those old men in Fawzi's office, dreaming about the wonderful things Merlin was going to do, with everything crumbling around them and everybody getting poorer every year, and doing nothing, nothing! And when you were coming home, I was expecting you to tell them there was no Merlin and to go to work and do something for themselves. But you didn't, and I couldn't see what you were trying to do. And then when Wade joined you and Father, I thought he was either helping you put over some kind of a swindle or else he'd started believing in Merlin himself. I should have seen what you were trying to do from the beginning. At least, from when you talked them into cleaning the town up and fixing the escalators and getting the fountains going again."

So the fountains weren't dusty any more.

"How's Mother taking things now?"

Flora looked distressed. "She goes around wringing her hands. Honestly. I never saw anybody doing that outside a soap opera. Half the time she thinks you and Father are a pair of unprincipled scoundrels, and the other half she thinks you're going to let Merlin destroy the world."

"I'm beginning to be afraid of something like that myself."

"Huh? But Merlin's just a big fake, isn't it? You're using it to make these people do something they wouldn't do for themselves, aren't you?"

"It started that way. What do you think all this is about?" he asked, gesturing toward the excavation and the two giant mining machines digging and blasting and pounding away at the rock.

"Well, to keep Kurt Fawzi and that crowd happy, I suppose. It seems like an awful waste of time, though."

"I'm afraid it isn't. I'm afraid Merlin, or something just

161

as bad, is down there. That's why I'm here, instead of on Koshchei. I want to keep people like Fawzi from doing anything foolish with it when they find it."

"But there *can't* be a Merlin!"

"I'm afraid there is. Not the sort of a Merlin Fawzi expects to find; that thing's too small for that. But there's something down there. . . ."

The question of size bothered him. That drum-shaped superstructure couldn't even hold the personnel-record machine they had found here, or the computers at the Storisende Stock Exchange. It could have been an intelligence-evaluator, or an enemy-intentions predictor, but it seemed small even for that. It would be something *like* a computer; that was as far as he was able to go. And it could be something completely outside the reach of his imagination.

At the back of his mind, the suspicion grew that Carl Leibert knew exactly what it was. And he became more and more convinced that he had seen the self-styled preacher before.

Finally, the whole top of the hundred-foot collapsium-covered structure was uncovered, and the excavation had been leveled out wide enough to accommodate all the massive paraphernalia of the collapsium-cutter. They put *The Thing* onto contragravity again, and brought her down in place; the work of lifting off the reactor and the converter and the rest of it, piece by piece, began. Finally, everything was set up.

A dozen and a half of them were gathered in the room that had become their meeting-place, after dinner. They were all too tired to start the cutting that night, and at the same time excited and anxious. They talked in disconnected snatches, and then somebody put on one of the telecast screens. A music program was just ending; there was a brief silence, and then a commentator appeared, identifying his news-service. He spoke rapidly and breathlessly, his professional gravity cracking all over.

"The hypership *City of Asgard,* from Aton, has just come into telecast range," he began. "We have received an ex-

162

clusive Interworld News Service story, recently brought to Aton on the Pan-Federation Spacelines ship *Magellanic,* from Terra.

"News of revived interest in the Third Force computer, Merlin, having reached Terra by way of Odin, representatives of Interworld News, to which this service subscribes, interviewed retired Force-General Foxx Travis, now living, at the advanced age of a hundred and fourteen, on Luna. General Travis, who commanded the Third Fleet-Army Force here during the War, categorically denied that there had ever existed any super-computer of the sort.

"We bring you, now, a recorded interview with General Travis, made on Luna . . ."

For an instant, Conn felt the room around him whirling dizzily, and then he caught hold of himself. Everybody else was shouting in sudden consternation, and then everybody was hushing everybody else and making twice as much noise. The screen flickered; the commentator vanished, and instead, seated in the deep-cushioned chair, was the thin and frail old man with whom Conn had talked two years before, and through an open segment of the dome-roof behind him the full Earth shone, the continents of the Western Hemisphere plainly distinguishable. A young woman in starchy nurse's white bent forward solicitously from beside the chair, handing him a small beaker from which he sipped some stimulant. He looked much as he had when Conn had talked to him. But there was something missing . . .

Oh, yes. The comparative youngster of seventy-some— "Mike Shanlee . . . my *aide-de-camp* on Poictesme . . . now he thinks he's my keeper . . ." He wasn't in evidence, and he should be. Then Conn knew where and when he had seen the man who claimed to be a preacher named Carl Leibert.

"There is absolutely no truth in it, gentlemen," Travis was saying. "There never was any such computer. I only wish there had been; it would have shortened the War by years. We did, of course, use computers of all sorts, but they were all the conventional types used by business organizations . . ."

The rest was lost in a new outburst of shouting; General Travis, in the screen, continued in dumb-show. The only

THE COSMIC COMPUTER

thing Conn could distinguish was Leibert's—Shanlee's—voice, screaming: "Can it be a lie? Is there no Great Computer?" Then Kurt Fawzi was pounding on the top of the desk and bellowing, "Shut up! Listen!"

"Frankly, I'm surprised," Travis was continuing. "Young Maxwell talked to me, here in this room, a couple of years ago; I told him then that nothing of the sort existed. If he's back on Poictesme telling people there is, he's lying to them and taking advantage of their credulity. There never was anything called Project Merlin . . ."

"Hah, who's a liar now?" Klem Zareff shouted. "Dolf, what did your people find in the Library?"

"Why, that's right!" Professor Kellton exclaimed. "My students did find a dozen references to Project Merlin. He couldn't be ignorant of anything like that."

"This youth has been lying to us all along!" the old man with the beard cried, pointing an accusing finger at Conn. "He has created false hopes; he has given us faith in a delusion. Why, he is the wickedest monster in human history!"

"Well, thank you, General Travis," another voice, from the screen-speaker, was saying. The only calm voice in the room. "That was a most excellent statement, sir. It should . . ."

"Conn, you didn't tell us you'd talked to General Travis," Morgan Gatworth was saying. "Why didn't you?"

"Because I never believed anything he told me. You were in Kurt Fawzi's office the day I came home; you know how shocked everybody was when I told you I hadn't been able to learn anything positive. Why should I repeat his lies and discourage everybody that much more? Why, he'd deny there was a Merlin if he was sitting on top of it," Conn declared. "He wants the credit for winning the War, not for letting Merlin win it for him."

"I don't blame Conn," Klem Zareff said. "If he'd told us that then, some of us might have believed it."

"And look what we found," Kurt Fawzi added, pointing at the ceiling. "Is that Merlin up there, or isn't it?"

"That little thing!" Shanlee cried scornfully. "How could that be Merlin? I am going to my chamber, to pray for forgiveness for this wretch."

164

He turned and started for the door.

"Stop him, Tom!" Conn said, and Tom Brangwyn put himself in front of the older man, gripping his right arm. Shanlee tried, briefly, to resist.

"Seems to me you lost faith in Merlin awfully quick," the former town marshal of Litchfield said. "You knew there was a Merlin all along, and you never wanted us to find it."

Franz Veltrin, who had been "Leibert's" most enthusiastic adherent, had also lost faith suddenly; he was shouting vituperation at the Prophet of Merlin.

"Knock it off, Franz; he was only doing his duty," Conn said. "Weren't you, General Shanlee?"

It took almost a minute before they stopped yelling for an explanation and allowed him to make one. He caught Klem Zareff's comment: "Must be pretty hot, if they have to send a general to handle it."

"I talked to Travis, yes. He gave me the same story he just repeated on that interview," Conn said, picking his way carefully between fact and fiction. "After I went back to Montevideo, he and this aide of his must have been afraid I didn't believe it, which I didn't. When I was ready to graduate, I got this offer of an instructorship; that was a bribe to keep me on Terra and off Poictesme. When I turned it down and took the *Mizar* home, Travis sent Shanlee after me. He must have grown that beard and that pageboy bob on the way out. I suppose he contacted Murchison as soon as he landed. Wait a minute."

He went to the communication screen and punched out a combination. A girl appeared and singsonged: "Barton-Massarra, Investigation and Protection."

"Conn Maxwell here. We gave you some audiovisuals of a man with a white beard, alias Carl Leibert," he began.

"Just a sec, Mr. Maxwell." She spoke quickly into a hand-phone. The screen flickered, and she was replaced by a hard-faced young man in dark clothes.

"Hello, Mr. Maxwell; Joe Massarra. We haven't anything on Leibert yet."

"Are any of the officers of the *Andromeda* where you can

165

contact them? Let them see those audiovisuals. I'll bet that beard was grown aboard ship coming out from Terra."

Bedlam broke out suddenly. Shanlee, who had been standing passively, his right arm loosely grasped by Tom Brangwyn, came down on Brangwyn's instep with the heel of his left foot and hit Brangwyn under the chin with the heel of his left palm. Wrenching his arm free, he started for the door. Sylvie Jacquemont snatched a chair and threw it along the floor; it hit the fleeing man's ankles and brought him down. Half a dozen men piled on top of him, and Brangwyn was yelling to them not to choke him to death till he could answer some questions.

"Hey, what's going on?" the detective-agency man in the screen was asking. "Need help? We'll start a car right away."

"Everything's under control, thank you."

Massarra hesitated for a moment. "What's the dope on this statement that was on telecast a few minutes ago?" he asked.

"Travis doesn't want us to find Merlin. What you just heard was one of his people, planted here at Force Command. We're going to question him when we have time. But there isn't a word of truth in that statement you just heard on the *Herald-Guardian* newscast. Merlin exists, and we've found it. We'll have it opened inside of thirty hours at most."

That was the line he was going to take with everybody. As soon as he had Massarra off the screen, he was punching the combination of his father's private screen at Interplanetary Building. It took five interminable minutes before Rodney Maxwell came on. He could hear Klem Zareff shouting orders into one of the inside communication screens —general turnout, everything on combat-ready; guards to come at once to the office.

"How close are you to digging that thing out?" his father asked as soon as he appeared.

"We're down to it; we can start cutting the collapsium any time now."

"Start cutting it ten minutes ago," his father told him. "And don't leave Force Command till you have it open. How many men and vehicles does Klem have for defense?

166

You'll need all of them in a couple of hours. Everybody here is stunned, now; they'll come out of it inside an hour, and they'll come out fighting."

"You'd better come out here." He turned, saw Jerry Rivas helping hold Shanlee in a chair, and shouted to him: "Jerry! Turn out the workmen. Start cutting the can open right away." He turned back to his father. "Klem's just ordered all his force out. Are you coming here?"

"I can't. In about an hour, everything's going up with a bang. I have to be here to grab a few of the pieces."

"You'll do a lot of good in jail, or on the end of a rope."

"Chance I have to take," his father replied. "I think I'll have a couple of hours. If anybody from the press calls you, what are you going to tell them?"

Conn repeated the line he had taken already. His father nodded.

"All right. I'll call you later. If I can. Just keep things going at your end."

A dozen of Klem Zareff's men were crowding into the room.

"This man's under close arrest," the old soldier was telling them. "He is very important and very dangerous. Take him out somewhere, search him to the skin, take his clothes away from him and give him a robe. He's to be watched every second; make sure he hasn't poison or other suicide means. He's to be questioned later."

As soon as Rodney Maxwell was off the screen, there was a call-signal. It was one of the news-services, wanting a statement.

"I'll take it," Gatworth said, and then began talking:

"This statement of General Travis's is completely false. There is a Merlin, and we've found it . . ."

They found something that might be good-enough Merlin for the next thirty hours. That superstructure was just big enough for the manually operated parts of a computer like Merlin; the input and output, and the programming machines.

XX

KLEM ZAREFF'S guardsmen were mercenaries. A little over a year ago they had, at best, been homeless drifters, and not a few had been outlaws. Now they were soldiers, well fed, clothed, quartered and equipped, and well and regularly paid. They had a good thing; they were willing to fight to keep it, Merlin or no Merlin. Conn left them to their commander. He did gather the workmen for a short harangue, but that wasn't really necessary. They had a good thing, too, and most of them realized that they were working toward a better thing. They could be depended upon, too.

They came crowding out and manned lifters; they got the heavy collapsium-cutter maneuvered into place and the shielding down around the cutting-head. After that, there were only four men who could work, each in his own heavily shielded cabin. In spite of the shielding that covered the actual work, there was an awesome display of multicolored light; it was like being in the middle of an aurora borealis. What was going on where that tiny rotating beam of cosmic rays was grinding at the collapsium simply couldn't have been imagined.

Conn would have liked to stay outside; he could not. Too many things were happening in too many places, and it was all coming in by screen. Rioting had broken out in Storisende and in a dozen other places. He saw, on a news-screen, a mob raging in front of the Executive Palace; yellow-shirted Cybernarchists were battling with city police and Planetary troops, Armageddonists and Human Supremacy Leaguers were fighting both and one another. Above all the confused noise of shouting and shooting, an amplifier was braying: *"It's a lie! It's a lie! Merlin has been found!"*

Newsmen began arriving—Zareff's men had orders to pass them through the cordon that had been put up around Force Command—and they took up his time. It was worth it, though. They could tell him what was going on.

J. Fitzwilliam Sterber called. Rodney Maxwell had been arrested, on a farrago of fraud charges—"I don't know who he's supposed to have defrauded; the Planetary Government is the sole complainant"—and bail was being illegally denied. Sterber's lawyerly soul was outraged, but he was grimly elated. "You wait till things quiet down a little. We're going to start a false-arrest suit—"

"If you're alive to." Apparently Sterber hadn't thought of that. "What do you think's going to happen when the Stock Exchange opens?"

"It's going to be bad. But don't worry; your father must have foreseen something like this. He gave me instructions, and instructed a few more people." He named some of the Trisystem Investments people and some of the bankers. "We're going to try to brace the market as long as we can. Nobody who keeps his head is going to lose anything in the long run."

Luther Chen-Wong called from Port Carpenter, on Koshchei. He and Clyde Nichols and a young mathematics professor named Simon Macquarte had been running the colony, in Conn's absence and since Yves Jacquemont had gone to space in the *Ouroboros II.*

"Well, they caught up with you," he said. Evidently he had figured out what the search for Merlin was all about, too. "What do we do about it?"

"Well, we are just before finding Merlin, here. I hope we find it before things get too bad." He told Luther the situation of the moment. "Have you people started on another hyper-ship yet?"

"We're getting organized to. I don't suppose it's advisable to send any more ships in to Storisende for a while? And are you sure this thing you've found is Merlin?"

"I don't know what it is. It's only big enough for the apparatus they'd need to operate a thing like Merlin—Yes, Luther. I am sure we have found Merlin."

Chen-Wong looked at him curiously. "I hope so. I can't think of anything else that can stop this business."

Tom Brangwyn was in the room when he turned from the screen.

"We searched Leibert's—Shanlee's—rooms," he said. "We found a bomb."

"What kind of a bomb?"

"Vest-pocket thermonuclear. He seems to have gotten the fissionables by taking apart a couple of light tactical missiles; the whole thing's packed inside a hundred-pound power-cartridge case. It was in a traveling-bag under his bed. And you know how it was to be fired? With a regular 40-mm flare-pistol, welded into the end of the bomb. The flare-powder had been taken out of the cartridge, and it had been reloaded with a big charge of rifle-powder. I suppose it would blow one subcritical mass into another. But the only way he could have fired the bomb would have been by pulling the trigger."

And blowing himself up along with it. He must have wanted Merlin destroyed pretty badly.

"Have you questioned him yet?"

"Not yet. I wanted to tell you about it first."

He looked at his watch. Only four hours had passed since the newscast; why, that seemed like months, ago, now.

"All right, Tom; we'll go talk to him. Where's the Colonel?"

Zareff was surrounded by a dozen screens, keeping in touch with the *Lester Dawes* and the gunboats and combat cars, and the gun positions with which he had ringed Force Command. It was only a little army, maybe, but he was a busy commander-in-chief.

"You take care of it. Tell me what you get from him. I can't leave now. There's a report of a number of aircraft approaching from the west now . . ."

They found Judge Ledue, and Kurt Fawzi and Dolf Kellton, who were just sitting around wishing there was something to do to help. They gave Franz Veltrin and Sylvie Jacquemont the job of keeping the representatives of the

170

press amused. Then they went down to the room in which General Mike Shanlee was held under guard.

Shanlee, wearing a bathrobe and nothing else, was lying on a cot, sleeping peacefully; three of Zareff's men were sitting on chairs, watching him narrowly.

"All right; you can go," Conn told them. "We'll take care of him."

Shanlee woke instantly; he sat up and swung his legs over the edge of the cot.

"You have my name and rank," he said, and his voice no longer quavered. "My serial number is—" He recited a string of figures. "And that's all you're getting out of me."

"We'll get anything we want out of you," Conn told him. "You know what a mind-probe is? You should; your accomplices used one on my father's secretary. She's a hopeless imbecile now. You'll be, too, when we're through with you. But before then, you'll have given us everything you know."

Kellton began to protest. "Conn, you can't do a thing like that!"

"A mind-probe is utterly illegal; why, it's a capital offense!" Ledue exclaimed. "Conn I forbid you . . ."

"Judge, don't make me call those guards and have you removed," Conn said.

"You can stop bluffing," Shanlee told him. "Where would you get a mind-probe?"

"Out of the Chief of Intelligence's office, here in his headquarters. I should imagine it was to be used in interrogating Alliance prisoners, during the War. I think Colonel Zareff would enjoy helping to use it on you. He used to be an Alliance officer."

Shanlee was silent. Conn sat down in one of the chairs, at the small table.

"General Shanlee, would you describe General Foxx Travis as a man of honor and integrity? And would you so describe yourself?" Shanlee said nothing. "Yet both of you have lied, deliberately and repeatedly, to conceal the existence of Merlin. And we found that bomb in your room. You were willing to blow up this headquarters and everybody, yourself included, in it, to keep us from getting at

Merlin. Well, you know that we can make you tell us the truth, maybe when it's too late, and you know that we are going to get Merlin. We're cutting the collapsium off that thing above now."

Shanlee laughed. "You're supposed to be a computerman. You think that little thing could be Merlin?"

"The controls and programming machine for Merlin." He turned to Kurt Fawzi. "You always claimed that Merlin was here in Force Command. You had it backward. Force Command is inside Merlin."

"What do you mean, Conn?"

"The walls; the fifty-foot walls, shielded inside and out. Merlin—the circuitry, the memory-bank, the relays, everything—was installed inside them. What's up above is only what was needed to operate the computer. Isn't that true, General?"

Shanlee had stopped his derisive laughter. He sat on the edge of the cot, tensing as though for a leap at Conn's throat.

"That won't help, either. If you try it, we won't shoot you. We'll just overpower you and start mind-probing right away. Now; you feel that suppressing Merlin was worth any sacrifice. We're not unreasonable. If you can convince us that Merlin ought not to be brought to light . . . Well, you can't do any harm by talking, and you may do some good. You may even accomplish your mission."

"He can't talk us out of it," Kurt Fawzi seemed determined to spoil things by saying. "Conn, I'm coming around to Klem's way of thinking. They just don't want anybody else to have it."

"No, we don't," Shanlee said. "We don't want the whole Federation breaking up into bloody anarchy, and that's what'll happen if you dig that thing up and put it into operation."

Nobody said anything except Fawzi, who began an indignant contradiction and then subsided. Tom Brangwyn lit a cigarette.

"Would you mind letting me have one of those?" Shanlee said. "I haven't had a smoke since I came here. It wouldn't have been in character."

Brangwyn took one out of the pack, lit it at the tip of his own, and gave it to Shanlee with his left hand, his right ready to strike. Shanlee laughed in real amusement.

"Oh, Brother!" he reproved, in his former pious tones. "You distrust your fellow man; that is a sin."

He rose slowly, the bathrobe flapping at his bare shins, and sat down across the table from Conn.

"All right," he said. "I'll tell· you about it. I'll tell you the truth, which will be something of a novelty all around."

Shanlee puffed for a moment at the cigarette; it must really have tasted good after his long abstinence.

"You know, we were really caught off balance when the War ended. It even caught Merlin short; information lag, of course. The whole Alliance caved in all at once. Well, we fed Merlin all the data available, and analyzed the situation. Then we did something we really weren't called upon to do, because that was policy-planning and wasn't our province, but we were going to move an occupation army into System States planets, and we didn't want to do anything that would embarrass the Federation Government later. We fed Merlin every scrap of available information on political and economic conditions everywhere in the Federation, and set up a long-term computation of the general effects of the War.

"The extrapolation was supposed to run five hundred years in the future. It didn't. It stopped, at a point a trifle over two hundred years from now, with a statement that no computation could be made further because at that point the Terran Federation would no longer exist."

The others, who had taken chairs facing him, looked at him blankly.

"No more Federation?" Judge Ledue asked incredulously. "Why, the Federation, the Federation . . ."

The Federation would last forever. Anybody knew that. There just couldn't be no more Federation.

"That's right," Shanlee said. "We had trouble believing it, too. Remember, we were Federation officers. The Federation was our religion. Just like patriotism used to be, back in the days of nationalism. We checked for error. We made detail analyses. We ran it all over again. It was no use.

"In two hundred years, there won't be any Terran Federation. The Government will collapse, slowly. The Space Navy will disintegrate. Planets and systems will lose touch with Terra and with one another. You know what it was like here, just before the War? It will be like that on every planet, even on Terra. Just a slow crumbling, till everything is gone; then every planet will start sliding back, in isolation, into barbarism."

"Merlin predicted that?" Kurt Fawzi asked, shocked.

If Merlin said so, it had to be true.

Shanlee nodded. "So we ran another computation; we added the data of publication of this prognosis. You know, Merlin can't predict what you or I would do under given circumstances, but Merlin can handle large-group behavior with absolue accuracy. If we made public Merlin's prognosis, the end would come, not in two centuries but in less than one, and it wouldn't be a slow, peaceful decay; it would be a bomb-type reaction. Rebellions. Overthrow of Federation authority, and then revolt and counterrevolt against planetary authority. Division along sectional or class lines on individual planets. Interplanetary wars; what we fought the Alliance to prevent. Left in ignorance of the future, people would go on trying to make do with what they had. But if they found out that the Federation was doomed, everybody would be trying to snatch what they could, and end by smashing everything. Left in ignorance, there might be a planet here and there that would keep enough of the old civilization to serve, in five or so centuries, as a nucleus for a new one. Informed in advance of the doom of the Federation, they would all go down together in the same bloody shambles, and there would be a Galactic night of barbarism for no one knows how many thousand years."

"We don't want anything like that to happen!" Tom Brangwyn said, in a frightened voice.

"Then pull everybody out of here and blow the place up, Merlin along with it," Shanlee said.

"No! We'll not do that!" Fawzi shouted. "I'll shoot the man dead who tries it!"

"Why didn't you people blow Merlin up?" Conn asked.

"We'd built it; we'd worked with it. It was part of us, and we were part of it. We couldn't. Besides, there was a chance that it might survive the Federation; when a new civilization arose, it would be useful. We just sealed it. There were fewer than a hundred of us who knew about it. We all took an oath of secrecy. We spent the rest of our lives trying to suppress any mention of Merlin or the Merlin Project. You have no idea how shocked both General Travis and I were when you told us that the story was still current here on Poictesme. And when we found that you'd been getting into the records of the Third Force, I took the next ship I could, a miserable little freighter, and when I landed and found out what was happening, I contacted Murchison and scared the life out of him with stories about a secessionist conspiracy. All this Armageddonist, Human Supremacy, Merlin-is-the-Devil, stuff that's been going on was started by Murchison. And he succeeded in scaring Vyckhoven with the Cybernarchists, too."

"This computation on the future of the Federation is still in the back-work file?" Conn asked.

Shanlee nodded. "We were criminally reckless; I can see that, now. Let me beg, again, that you destroy the whole thing."

"We'll have to talk it over among ourselves," Judge Ledue said. "The five of us, here, cannot presume to speak for everybody. We will, of course, have to keep you confined; I hope you will understand that we cannot accept your parole."

"Is there anything you want in the meantime?" Conn asked.

"I would like something to smoke, and some clothes," General Shanlee said. "And a shave and a haircut."

XXI

ALL THROUGH the night, a shifting blaze of many-colored light rose and dimmed the stars above the mesa. They stared in awe, marveling at the energy that was pouring out of the converters into a tiny spot that inched its way around the collapsium shielding. It must have been visible for hundreds of miles; it was, for there was a new flood of rumors circulating in Storisende and repeated and denied by the newscasts, now running continuously. Merlin had been found. Merlin had been blown up by Government troops. Merlin was being transported to Storisende to be installed as arbiter of the Government. Merlin the Monster was destroying the planet. Merlin the Devil was unchained.

Conn and Kurt Fawzi and Dolf Kellton and Judge Ledue and Tom Brangwyn clustered together, talking in whispers. They had told nobody, yet, of the interview with Shanlee.

"You think it would make all that trouble?" Kellton was asking anxiously, hoping that the others would convince him that it wouldn't.

"Maybe we had better destroy it," Judge Ledue faltered. "You see what it's done already; the whole planet's in anarchy. If we let this go on . . ."

"We can't decide anything like that, just the five of us," Brangwyn was insisting. "We'll have to get the others together and see what they think. We have no right to make any decision like this for them."

"They're no more able to make the decision than we are," Conn said.

"But we've got to; they have a right to know . . ."

"If you decide to destroy Merlin, you'll have to decide to kill me, first," Kurt Fawzi said, his voice deadly calm. "You won't do it while I'm alive."

"But, Kurt," Ledue expostulated. "You know why these people here at Storisende are rioting? It's because they've lost hope, because they're afraid and desperate. The Terran Federation is something everybody feels they have to have, for peace and order and welfare. If people thought it was breaking up, they'd be desperate, too. They'd do the same insane things these people here on this planet are doing. General Shanlee was right. Don't destroy the hope that keeps them sane."

"We don't need to do that," Kurt Fawzi argued. "We can use Merlin to solve our own problems; we don't need to tell the whole Federation what's going to happen in two hundred years."

"It would get out; it couldn't help getting out," Ledue said.

"Let's not try to decide it ourselves," Conn said. "Let's get Merlin into operation, and run a computation on it."

"You mean, ask Merlin to tell us whether it ought to be destroyed or not?" Ledue asked incredulously. "Let Merlin put itself on trial, and sentence itself to destruction?"

"Merlin is a computer; computers deal only in facts. Computers are machines; they have no sense of self-preservation. If Merlin ought to be destroyed, Merlin will tell us so."

"You willing to leave it up to Merlin, Kurt?" Tom Brangwyn asked.

Fawzi gulped. "Yes. If Merlin says we ought to, we'll have to do it."

Toward noon, a telecast went out from Koshchei, on a dozen different wave-lengths. Conn, half asleep in a chair in the commander-in-chief's office, saw Simon Macquarte, the young mathematics professor from Storisende College who had become one of the leaders of the colony, appear in the screen. The next moment, he was fully awake, shocked by Macquarte's words:

"This is not a threat; this is a solemn, even a prayerful, warning. We do not want to use genocidal weapons of mass destruction against the world of our birth. But whether we do or not rests solely with you.

"We came here with a dream of a better world, a world of happiness and plenty for all. We have been working, on Koshchei, to build such a world on Poictesme. Now you are smashing that dream. When it is gone, we will have nothing to live for—except revenge. And we will take that revenge, make no mistake.

"We have the weapons with which to take it. Remember, this was a Federation naval base and naval arsenal during the War. Here the Federation Navy built their super-missiles, the missiles which devastated Ashmodai, and Belphegor, and Baphomet, and hundreds of these weapons are here. We have them, ready for launching. Once they are launched, with the robo-pilots set for targets on Poictesme, you will have a hundred and sixty hours, at the most, to live.

"We will launch them immediately if there is another attack made upon Force Command Duplicate HQ, or upon Interplanetary Building in Storisende, or if Rodney Maxwell is killed, no matter by whom or under what circumstances.

"We beg you, earnestly and prayerfully, not to force us to do this dreadful thing. We speak to each one of you, for each one of you holds the fate of the planet in his own hands."

The image faded from the screen. As it did, Conn was looking from one to another of the people in the room with him. All were dumbfounded, most of them frightened.

"They wouldn't do it, would they?" Lorenzo Menardes was asking. "Conn, you know those people. They wouldn't really?"

"Don't depend on it, Lorenzo," Klem Zareff said. "It's hard for a lot of people to shoot somebody ten feet away with a pistol. But just sending off a missile; that's nothing but setting a lot of dials and then pushing a button."

"I'm not worrying about whether they'd do it or not," Conn said. "What I'm worrying about is how many people will believe they will."

Apparently a good many people did. Zareff's combat vehicles began reporting a cessation of fighting. The newscasts, repeating the ultimatum from Koshchei, told of fewer and fewer disorders in the city or elsewhere; by midafternoon, the rioting had stopped.

By that time, too, Rodney Maxwell was on-screen. He was, Conn noticed, wearing his pistols again.

"What happened?" he asked. "They let you out on bail?"

Maxwell shook his head. "Charges dismissed; they didn't have anything to charge me with in the first place. But they haven't let me out yet."

"You're wearing your guns."

"Yes, but they still have me penned up here at the Executive Palace; they're practically keeping me in the safe. I wish our people on Koshchei hadn't mentioned me in their ultimatum; Jake Vyckhoven's afraid to let me run around loose for fear some lunatic shoots me and starts the planet-busters coming in. Jake did one good thing, though. He ordered the Stock Exchange closed, and declared a five-day bank holiday. By that time, you ought to have Merlin opened and working, and then the market'll be safe."

Conn simply replied, "I hope so." There was no telling what kind of taps there might be on the screen his father was using; he couldn't risk telling him about Shanlee, or about the last computation which Merlin had made. "If we send the *Lester Dawes* in, do you think you might talk them into letting you come out here?"

"I can try."

Flora arrived at Force Command that afternoon.

"I would have come sooner," she said, "but Mother's had a complete collapse. It happened last evening; she's in the hospital. I was with her until just an hour and a half ago. She's still unconscious."

"You mean she's in danger?"

"I don't know. They think she's all right, except for the shock. It was the Travis statement that did it."

"Think I ought to go to her?"

Flora shook her head. "Just keep on with what you're doing here. There isn't anything you can do for her now."

"The best thing you can do for her, Conn, is prove that you weren't lying about Merlin," Sylvie told him.

The *Lester Dawes* didn't make it from Force Command to Storisende and back until after dark, and the green and white and red and orange lights were rising in folds and waves. Rodney Maxwell had heard about his wife's condition; it was the first thing he spoke of when Conn and Flora and Sylvie met him as he got off the ship.

"There isn't anything we can do, Father," Flora said. "They'll call us when there's any change."

He said the same thing Sylvie had said. "The only thing we can do is get that infernal thing uncovered. Once we do this, everything'll be all right. We'll show your mother that it isn't a fake and it isn't anything dangerous; we'll put a stop to all these horror-stories about mechanical devils and living machines . . ."

Conn drew his father off where the girls couldn't overhear.

"This is something worse," he said. "This is a bomb that could blow up the whole Federation."

"Are you going nuts, too?" his father demanded.

Conn told him about Shanlee; he repeated, almost word for word, the story Shanlee had told.

"Do you believe that?" his father asked.

"Don't you? You were in Storisende when the Travis statement came out; you saw how people acted. If this story gets out, people will be acting the same way on every planet in the Federation. Not just places like Poictesme; planets like Terra and Baldur and Marduk and Odin and Osiris. It would be the end of everything civilized, everywhere."

"Why didn't they use Merlin to save the Federation?"

"It's past saving. It's been past saving since before the War. The War was what gave it the final shove. If they could have used Merlin to reverse the process, they wouldn't have sealed it away."

"But you know, Conn, we can't destroy Merlin. If we did, the same people who went crazy over the Travis statement would go crazy all over again, worse than ever. We'd be destroying everything we planned for, and we'd be destroying ourselves. That bluff young Macquarte and Luther Chen-Wong and Bill Nichols made wouldn't work twice. And if they weren't bluffing . . ."

His father shuddered.

"And if we don't, how long do you think civilization will last here, if it blows up all over the rest of the Federation?"

The big machine cut on, a little spot of raw energy grinding away the collapsium, inch by inch; the undulating curtains of colored light illuminated the Badlands for miles around. Then, when the first hint of dawn came into the east, they went out. The steady roar of the generators that had battered every ear for over twenty-four hours stopped. There was unbelieving silence, and then shouts.

The workmen swarmed out to man lifters. Slowly the heavy apparatus—the reactor and the converters, the cutting machine, and the shielding around it—was lifted away. Finally, a lone lifter came in and men in radiation-suits went down to hook on grapples, and it lifted away, carrying with it a ten-foot-square sheet of thin steel that weighed almost thirty tons.

When they had battered a hole in the vitrified rock underneath, guards brought up General Shanlee. Somebody almost up to professional standards had given him a haircut; the beard was gone, too. A Federation Army officer's uniform had been found reasonably close to his size, and somebody had even provided him with the four stars of his retirement rank. He was, again, the man Conn had seen in the dome-house on Luna.

"Well, you got it open," he said, climbing down from the airjeep that had brought him. "Now, what are you going to do with it?"

"We can't make up our minds," Conn said. "We're going to let the computer tell us what to do with it."

Shanlee looked at him, startled. "You mean, you're going to have Merlin judge itself and decide its own fate?" he asked. "You'll get the same result we did."

They let a ladder down the hole and descended—Conn and his father, Kurt Fawzi, Jerry Rivas, then Shanlee and his two guards, then others—until a score of them were crowded in the room at the bottom, their flashlights illuminating the circular chamber, revealing ceiling-high metal cabinets, banks of button- and dial-studded control panels, big keyboards. It was Shanlee who found the lights and put them on.

"Powered from the central plant, down below," he said.

"The main cables are disguised as the grounding-outlet. If this thing had been on when you put on the power, you'd have had an awful lot of power going nowhere, apparently."

Rodney Maxwell was disappointed. "I know this stuff looks awfully complex, but I'd have expected there to be more of it."

"Oh, I didn't get a chance to tell you about that. This is only the operating end," Conn said, and then asked Shanlee if there were inspection-screens. When Shanlee indicated them, he began putting them on. "This is the real computer."

They all gave the same view, with minor differences—long corridors, ten feet wide, between solid banks of steel cabinets on either side. Conn explained where they were, and added:

"Kurt and the rest of them were sitting here, all this time, wondering where Merlin was; it was all around them."

"Well, how did you get up here?" Fawzi asked. "We couldn't find anything from below."

"No, you couldn't." Shanlee was amused. "Watch this."

It was so simple that nobody had ever guessed it. Below, back of the commander-in-chief's office, there was a closet, fifteen feet by twenty. They had found it empty except for some bits of discarded office-gear, and had used it as a catch-all for everything they wanted out of the way. Shanlee went to where four thick steel columns rose from floor to ceiling in a rectangle around a heavy-duty lifter, pressing a button on a control-box on one of them. The lifter, and the floor under it, rose, with a thick mass of vitrified rock underneath. The closet, full of the junk that had been thrown into it, followed.

"That's it," he said. "We just tore out the controls inside that and patched it up a little. There's a sheet of collapsium-plate under the floor. Your scanners simply couldn't detect anything from below."

Confident that Merlin would decree its own destruction, Shanlee gave his parole; the others accepted it. The newsmen were admitted to the circular operating room and encouraged to send out views and descriptions of everything. Then the lift controls were reinstalled, the lid was put back on top, and the only access to the room was through the office below. The entrance to this was always guarded by Zareff's soldiers or Brangwyn's police.

There were only a score of them who could be let in on the actual facts. For the most part, they were the same men who had been in Fawzi's office on the afternoon of Conn's return, a year and a half ago. A few others—Anse Dawes, Jerry Rivas, and five computermen Conn had trained on Koshchei—had to be trusted. Conn insisted on letting Sylvie Jacquemont in on the revised Awful Truth About Merlin. They spent a lot of their time together, in Travis's office, for the most part sunk in dejection.

They had finally found Merlin; now they most lose it. They were trying to reconcile themselves and take comfort from the achievement, empty as it was. They could see no way out. If Merlin said that Merlin had to be destroyed, that was it. Merlin was infallible. Conn hated the thought of destroying that machine with his whole being, not because it was an infallible oracle, but because it was the climactic masterpiece of the science he had spent years studying. To destroy it was an even worse sacrilege to him than it was to the Merlinolators. And Rodney Maxwell was thinking of the public effects. What the Travis statement had started would be nothing by comparison.

"You know, we can keep the destruction of Merlin a secret," Conn said. "It'll take some work down at the power plant, but we can overload all the circuits and burn everything out at once." He turned to Shanlee. "I don't know why you people didn't think of that."

Shanlee looked at him in surprise. "Why, now that you mention it, neither do I," he admitted. "We just didn't."

"Then," Conn continued, "we can tinker up something in the operating room that'll turn out what will look like computation results. As far as anybody outside ourselves will know, Merlin will still be solving everybody's problems. We'll do like any fortuneteller; tell the customer what he wants to believe and keep him happy."

More lies; lies without end. And now he'd have a machine to do his lying for him, a dummy computer that wouldn't compute anything. And all he'd wanted, to begin with, had been a ship to haul some brandy to where they could get a fair price for it.

Peace had returned. At first, it had been a frightened and uneasy peace. The bluff—he hoped that was what it had been—by the Koshchei colonists had shocked everybody into momentary inaction. In the twenty-four hours that had followed, the forces of sanity and order had gotten control again. Merlin existed and had been found. As for Travis's statement, the old general had been bound by a wartime oath of secrecy to deny Merlin's existence. The majority relaxed, ashamed of their hysterical reaction. As for the Cybernarchists and Armageddonists and Human Supremacy Leaguers, government and private police, vastly augmented by volunteers, speedily rounded up the leaders; their followers dispersed, realizing that Merlin was nothing but a lot of dials and buttons, and interestedly watching the broadcast views of it.

The banks were still closed, but discreet back-door withdrawals were permitted to keep business going; so was the Stock Exchange, but word was going around the brokerage offices that Trisystem Investments was in the market for a long list of securities. Nobody was willing to do anything that might upset the precarious balance; everybody was talking about the bright future, when Merlin would guide Poictesme to ever greater and more splendid prosperity.

Conn's father and sister flew to Litchfield; Flora stayed with her mother, and Rodney Maxwell returned to Force Command, shaking his head gravely.

"She's still unconscious, Conn," he said. "She just lies there, barely breathing. The doctors don't know . . . I wish Wade hadn't gone on the ship."

The price of what he had wanted to do was becoming unendurably high for Conn.

They ran off the computations Merlin had made forty years before, and rechecked them. There had been no error. The Terran Federation, overextended, had been cracking for a century before the War; the strain of that conflict had started an irreversible breakup. Two centuries for the

184

Federation as such; at most, another century of irregular trade and occasional war between independent planets, Galaxy full of human-populated planets as poor as Poictesme at its worst. Or, aware of the future, sudden outbursts of desperate violence, then anarchy and barbarism.

It took a long time to set up the new computation. Forty years of history for almost five hundred planets had to be abstracted and summarized and translated from verbal symbols to the electro-mathematical language of computers and fed in. Conn and Sylvie and General Shanlee and the three men and two women Conn had taught on Koshchei worked and rested briefly and worked again. Finally, it was finished.

"General; you're the oldest Merlin hand," Conn said, gesturing to the red button at the main control panel. "You do it."

"You do it, Conn. None of us would be here except for you."

"Thank you, General."

He pressed the button. They all stood silently watching the output slot.

Even a positronic computer does not work instantaneously. Nothing does. Conn took his eyes from the slot from which the tape would come, and watched the second-hand of the clock above it. The wait didn't seem like hours to him; it only seemed like seventy-five seconds, that way. Then the bell rang, and the tape began coming out.

It took another hour and a half of button-punching; the Braille-like symbols on the tape had to be retranslated, and even Merlin couldn't do that for itself. Merlin didn't think in human terms.

It was the same as before. In ignorance, the peoples of the Federation worlds would go on, striving to keep things running until they wore out, and then sinking into apathetic acceptance. Deprived of hope, they would turn to frantic violence and smash everything they most wanted to preserve. Conn pushed another button.

The second information-request went in: *What is the best course to be followed under these conditions by the people of Poictesme?* It had taken some time to phrase that in symbols a computer would find comprehensible; the answer, at great length, emerged in two minutes eight seconds. Re-translating it took five hours.

In the beginning and for the first ten years, it was, almost item for item, the Maxwell Plan. Export trade, specialized in luxury goods. Brandies and wines, tobacco; a long list of other exportable commodities, and optimum markets. Re-opening of industrial plants; establishment of new industries. Attainment of economic self-sufficiency. Cultural self-sufficiency; establishment of universities, institutes of technology, research laboratories. Then the Maxwell Plan became the Merlin Plan; the breakup of the Federation was a fact that entered into the computation. Build-up of military strength to resist aggression by other planetary governments. Defense of the Gartner Trisystem. Lists of possible aggressor planets. Revival of interstellar communications and trade; expeditions, conquest and re-education of natives . . .

"We can't begin to handle this without Merlin," Conn said. "If that means blowing up the Federation, let it blow. We'll start a new one here."

"No; if there's a general, violent collapse of the Federation, it'll spread to Poictesme," Shanlee told him. "Let's ask Merlin the big question."

Merlin took a good five minutes to work that one out. The question had to include a full description of Merlin, and a statement of the information which must be kept secret. The answer was even more lengthy, but it was summed up in the first word: *Falsification*.

"So Merlin's got to be a liar, too, along with the rest of us!" Sylvie cried. "Conn, you've corrupted his morals!"

The rest of it was false data which must be taped in, and lists of corrections which must be made in evaluating any computation into which such data might enter. There was also a statement that, after fifty years, suppression of the truth and circulation of falsely optimistic statements about the Federation would no longer have any importance.

"Well, that's it," Conn said. "Merlin thought himself out of a death sentence."

They crowded into the lift and went down to the office

THE COSMIC COMPUTER

below. Everybody who knew what had been going on upstairs was there. Most of them were nursing drinks; almost everybody was smoking. All of them were silent, until Judge Ledue took his cigar from his mouth.

"Has the jury reached a verdict?" he asked, clinging with courtroom formality to his self-control.

"Yes, your Honor. We find the defendant, Merlin, not guilty as charged."

In the uproar his words released, Rodney Maxwell got to his feet and came quickly to Conn.

"Flora called just a while ago. Your mother is conscious; she's asking for us. Flora says she seems perfectly normal."

"We'll go right away; take a recon-car. General, will you explain things till I get back? Sylvie, do you want to come with us?"

XXII

It was autumn again, the second autumn since he had landed from the *City of Asgard* at Storisende and taken the *Countess Dorothy* home to Litchfield. Again the fields were bare and brown; all up and down the Gordon Valley the melons were harvested, and the wine-pressing was ready to start.

The house was crowded today. All top-level Litchfield seemed to have turned out, and there were guests from Storisende, and even a few who had made the trip from Koshchei to be there. Simon Macquarte, the president of Koshchei Tech; Conn would always remember him in the screen threatening a whole planet with devastation. Luther Chen-Wong, the chief executive of Koshchei Colony. Clyde Nichols, the president of Koshchei Airlines.

He almost bumped into Yves Jacquemont, coming in from the hall. Jacquemont's beard had been trimmed down to a small imperial, and he was wearing the uniform of Trisystem & Interstellar Spacelines, nothing at all like a Federation

Space Navy uniform. He was laughing about something; he threw an arm over Conn's shoulder, and they went into the front parlor together.

"Oh, Gehenna of a big crop!" he heard Klem Zareff's voice, chuckling happily, above the babble in the room. "You wouldn't believe it. Why, we had to build six new vats . . ."

The thin-faced, white-haired man in the chair beside him said something. Mike Shanlee and Klem Zareff, old enemies, were not fast friends. Shanlee had come in from Force Command with Conn that morning. He had stayed on Poictesme as nominal head of Project Merlin, and intended to remain there for the rest of his life.

"Oh, there aren't any more farm-tramps," Zareff replied. "Everybody's getting factory jobs off-planet. I have an awful time getting help, and what I can get won't work for less than ten sols a day. Why, they're even organizing a union . . ."

There were feminine shrieks from across the room, and a stampede. The housecleaning-robot had come in, running its vacuum-cleaning hose around and brandishing its mops. He saw his mother break away from a group of older ladies and shout:

"*Oscar!*"

The robot stopped dead. "Yash'm?" a voice came out of it, Sheshan-accented.

"Go out!" his mother commanded. "Go to kitchen. Stay there."

"Yash'm." The robot floated out the door to the hall.

His mother rejoined her friends. Probably telling them, for the thousandth time, that her boy Conn fixed up the sound receptors and voice for Oscar. Or harping on how Conn had been telling everybody the truth, all along, and people wouldn't believe it.

Sylvie came up to him and caught his arm. "Come on, Conn; they're going to start the rehearsal," she said.

"They've been going to start it for an hour," her father told her.

"Well, they're really going to start it now."

188

"All right. You two run along," Yves Jacquemont said. "And you'd better start rehearsing for your own wedding before long. The *Genji* will be ready to hyper out in another month, and I don't want to be at space when my only daughter gets married."

They pushed through the crowd, dragging Conn's mother with them toward the big living room beyond. On the way, Mrs. Maxwell stopped to try to drag Judge Ledue out of a chair.

"Judge, the rehearsal is starting; they can't do it without you."

Ledue clung to his chair. "They daren't do it with me, Mrs. Maxwell. If I get into it, it won't be a rehearsal; they'll be really married, and then there won't be any point in having a wedding tomorrow."

"Oh, Morgan!" Conn called across the room to Gatworth. "You've just been appointed temporary judge for the wedding rehearsal!"

There was a big crowd around Wade Lucas, in the next room; he was telling them about the voyage to Baldur, from which he had returned, and the one to Irminsul, with a cargo of arms, machine tools and contragravity vehicles, on which he and his bride would go for their honeymoon. There was another crowd around Flora; she was telling them about the new fashions on Baldur, which had been brought back on the *Ouroboros II*.

"Where's your father?" his mother was asking him. "He has to rehearse giving the bride away."

"Probably in his office. I'll go get him."

"You'll get into an argument with somebody and forget to come back," his mother said. "Sylvie, you go with him, and bring both of them back."

"When'll we have our wedding, Sylvie?" he asked as they went off together.

"Well, before Dad goes to Aditya with the *Genji*. That'll have to be in a month."

"Two weeks? That ought to be plenty of time to get ready, and let people recover from this one."

"Everybody's here now. Let's make it a double wedding tomorrow," she suggested.

He hadn't been prepared for that. "Well, I hadn't expected . . . Sure! Good idea!" he agreed.

There was a crowd in Rodney Maxwell's little office—Fawzi and some others, and some Storisende people. One of the latter was vociferating:

"Jake Vyckhoven's no good, and he never was any good!"

"Well, you have to admit, if he hadn't ordered the banks and the Stock Exchange closed that time, we'd have had a horrible panic—"

"Admit nothing of the kind! Jethro, you were there, you'll bear me out. About a dozen of us were at Executive Palace for hours, bullying him into that. Why, we almost had to twist one of his arms while he was signing the order with the other. And now he has the gall to run for re-election on the strength of his heroic actions at the time of the Travis Hoax!"

"I know who we want for President!" another Storisende man exclaimed. "He's right here in this room!"

"Yes!" Rodney Maxwell almost bellowed, before the other man could say anything else. "Here he is!" He grabbed Kurt Fawzi by the arm and yanked him to his feet. "Here's the man most responsible for finding Merlin; the man who first suggested sending my son Conn to Terra to school, the man who, more than anyone else, devoted his life to the search for Merlin, the man whose inextinguishable faith and indomitable courage kept that search alive through its darkest hours. Everybody, get a drink; a toast to our next President, Kurt Fawzi!"

Conn was sure he heard his father add: "Ghu, what a narrow escape!"

Then he and Sylvie began chanting, in unison, *"We want Fawzi! We want Fawzi!"*

If you enjoyed this novel, you will also want to read:

SPACE VIKING

by

H. BEAM PIPER

After a galaxy-wide war had left the planetary federation in ruins, every surviving civilized world was on its own. And that was a perfect setup for the marauders from the far-out rim.

Trask was one of those dreaded Space Vikings, a warrior spaceman with a crew and a ship that struck terror to a thousand worlds. But Trask had a special personal interest in scourging the stars—he wanted to draw upon himself the fire of a certain enemy—a renegade planet-wrecker with a yen for galactic empire building.

Ace Book F-225   40¢

Here's a quick checklist of recent releases of
ACE SCIENCE-FICTION BOOKS

40¢

If you are missing any of these, they can be obtained
directly from the publisher by sending the indicated sum,
plus 5¢ handling fee, to Ace Books, Inc. (Dept. M M),
1120 Avenue of the Americas, New York, N.Y. 10036